PRAISE FOR THE ROXY REINHARDT MYSTERIES

"This second book in the series was so much fun!"

"Good clean read that is entertaining and piques the reader's interest."

"This is now one of my favorite series!"

"Good clean read that is entertaining and piques the reader's interest."

"I read your book until the wee hours last night.... couldn't put it down!!"

"All the food made me very hungry and really wanting to visit New Orleans!"

"Absolutely loved it!!!"

"You've done a great job. Truly. This one shines."

"I just want you to know how much I like Roxy. She makes me smile."

"Loved the book, looking forward to the next installment. I think you've got a winner!"

"I like Roxy and her new friends and look forward to more books including them."

"Love Roxy's posse."

"What a great book!"

NEW ORLEANS
NIGHTMARE

BOOKS IN THE ROXY REINHARDT MYSTERIES

Mardi Gras Madness

New Orleans Nightmare

Louisiana Lies

Cajun Catastrophe

COLLECTIONS

Books 1-3

Mardi Gras Madness

New Orleans Nightmare

Louisiana Lies

Published by Mesa Verde Publishing
P.O. Box 1002
San Carlos, CA 94070

ISBN: 978-0988795556

"A book, too can be a star, a living fire to lighten the darkness, leading out into the expanding universe."
- Madeline L'Engle -

NEW ORLEANS NIGHTMARE

ALISON GOLDEN

HONEY BROUSSARD

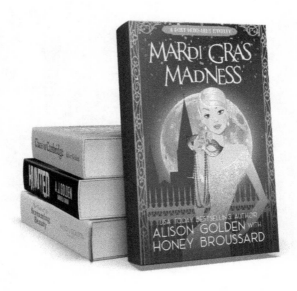

"Your emails seem to come on days when I need to read them because they are so upbeat."
- Linda W -

For a limited time, you can get the first books in each of my series - *Chaos in Cambridge, Hunted* (exclusively for subscribers - not available anywhere else), *The Case of the Screaming Beauty, and Mardi Gras Madness* - plus updates about new releases, promotions, and other Insider exclusives, by signing up for my mailing list at:

https://www.alisongolden.com/roxy

CHAPTER ONE

"OOOOH, I'M SO excited!" Roxy Reinhardt said, dancing around the kitchen, while pots and pans of all sizes bubbled on the stovetop. Gumbos, stews, and jambalayas filled the room with rich, spicy steam as she boogied in the space between the range and the countertops.

"Me too!" Nat said, clapping her hands together.

Roxy was the manager and part-owner of the Funky Cat Inn, having been recently installed as such by the previous owner, Evangeline, and local investor, laundry-man, handyman, and something of a handsome dark horse, Sam. Nat was Roxy's "Girl Friday." She was also a former English nanny who had overstayed her visa. Today they were preparing a "Grand Welcome Meal."

"Who are these people again?" Evangeline asked Roxy, for the third time. "I don't understand all these new-fangled Instabook things, cher."

Evangeline was retired and living her own life now, but she still came over to help them with the food. She was an absolute master at Creole and Cajun cooking and baking, and Roxy and Nat had submitted themselves to an extended tutelage.

"They're called influencers," Roxy explained. "That means that they have a lot of followers on Instagram."

"Huh?" Evangeline said.

Nat rolled her eyes and gave Roxy a wink as she looked back from a pot of gumbo she was stirring. "Instagram is a platform where you have your own page, and you put pictures on it. If people like what they see, they follow you to watch what you're going to put up next. We have a page for the Funky Cat. Sage runs it."

"So why are these . . ." Evangeline frowned. "Why are these influgrammers comin' here?"

"*Influencers,* Evangeline," Nat said.

Roxy laughed. "Influgrammers sounds pretty good, though! You might have just coined a new word there, Evangeline. Anyway, the influencers are coming here to stay as part of a promotion. We pay them to showcase their visit. All the pictures and videos they shoot while they are here get put on their Instagram feed, and their followers will see them. Since they have hundreds of thousands of followers, it's great publicity. This is huge for us."

Roxy had arrived in New Orleans during Mardi Gras season. Now though, spring had brightened into summer and the vivid colors and excitement of Mardi Gras were over. The city had lazily tilted into June, but with the imminent arrival of the influencers, the atmosphere at the Funky Cat was ramping up to a level never experienced in the building's entire 102-year existence.

Evangeline sighed, shaking her head with bemusement. "Back in my day, people simply bought an ad in a magazine or two."

Well into her eighties, Evangeline bustled around the

kitchen with pots and spices, her floral wraparound dresses swishing beneath her aprons as she did so. She was a flurry of bustle and action. She could still manage six pans on the flame at one time, and ordered Roxy and Nat about the place as if she still owned the kitchen, which, when she was in it, she did.

Nat picked up a large sack of crawfish and carried it into the back room to begin purging them. "Times have changed, Evangeline, and we've gotta keep up if we want the Funky Cat to be a success."

"It only has six rooms!" Evangeline cried, rearranging bags of spices on the counter. "How much of a success can it be?"

Roxy felt awkward. She didn't want to talk about how much more upscale the boutique hotel was now or how expensive the rooms had become since Evangeline's time as owner; it would be rude and embarrassing.

"Well, the room rates are just a touch higher, so we need a new, more affluent demographic, that's all. Now, shouldn't we get started on the jalapeño cornbreads? Where have those ramekins gotten to?"

They were really going to town on the welcome meal for the influencers. It was to be a five-course affair.

"Do you think they'll be able to eat all this lot?" Nat wondered out loud as she wandered back into the kitchen a few minutes later. She was carrying a pot of newly purged crawfish with a grin on her face. "For course one, we've got a chicken gumbo with Cajun spices." Nat ladled up a spoonful of the gumbo and let it slowly pour back into the pan. "Followed by miniature crawfish and cheese pies, followed by Shrimp Creole. That's shrimp cooked in tomatoes, peppers and hot sauce, with white rice, Roxy," the young English woman said gravely.

Nat was a Funky Cat treasure. She helped Roxy with anything that was needed at the boutique hotel, from cooking to serving guests, from checking them in to cleaning their rooms. And her talents extended even further. Nat possessed a voice that was so smooth and creamy that Roxy had hired her on the spot to sing for guests.

Now, Nat's black nail polish gleamed in the lights of the kitchen. Her excitement about the upcoming meal really *was* something. Getting the cynical, skeptical Nat to be joyous and upbeat about anything was a true feat. But then, what was coming was a bold, new experiment for the small hotel.

"Yum, and I'm preparing dessert—warm bread pudding with caramel and whiskey sauce," Roxy said.

"Don't forget the cheese course!" Evangeline cried out from where she was stirring a huge pot of broth.

"I'm not sure they will be able to eat it all, but I do know that thousands and thousands will be watching via their Instagram accounts, and we have to give a great impression, not only of the Funky Cat, but of New Orleans," Roxy finished.

The city was the first place Roxy had ever felt truly at home. It was hard to explain, but New Orleans had gotten into her bones somehow. There was a *heat* about "N'awlins" as the locals called it, perhaps from the spices, perhaps from the carnivals and the magic and the spiritualism that lurked about the place, perhaps from the music that floated from basements and businesses at any time of the day or night. Whatever it was, the essence of it had found its way into Roxy's very soul, lodged itself there, and wasn't about to leave any time soon.

As she chopped onions and garlic for the Shrimp Creole, Roxy sighed happily to herself. Things were *finally* falling into place in her life, and she felt cozy and warm and safe. Just then, they heard the sound of the front door knocker being rapped. Hard.

Roxy frowned, her knife paused over an onion. She was expecting Sam, but he'd have simply walked in without knocking. Roxy wiped her hands down her apron and hurried out of the kitchen, through the dining room and into the hallway. The influencers weren't due for a good three hours. She hoped this wasn't one of them arriving early. She wanted to be dressed in her best and have the food ready before they got even so much as a glimpse of the Funky Cat or its proprietor. A little flustered, she pulled open the door. Her heart sank.

A very tall, slim woman with huge sunglasses and long, black hair that cascaded in waves down her back stood on the doorstep. She wore chunky high heels on her feet, skinny jeans, and a leather jacket with a fur collar that looked very expensive indeed. Behind her, six Louis Vuitton suitcases and two holdalls were piled up in the courtyard. Without so much as a greeting, the woman walked assuredly past Roxy and into the Funky Cat lobby.

"Oh, hello," Roxy said, stepping back to give the woman room to pass. *Who was she?* The woman had walked in like *she* owned the place, a demeanor that Roxy suspected was her visitor's default setting. Then she remembered who the woman was!

"Good afternoon," the visitor said, pushing her sunglasses on top of her head. "I am Ada Okafor." The woman eyed Roxy. "But I expect you knew that. I'm early, I know. I'm always early. The early bird catches the worm. Snooze, you lose." She flicked her wrist and poked one forefinger into the air.

Roxy recovered quickly. "Great to meet you. I'm Roxy

Reinhardt, part-owner and manager of this hotel." Roxy stuck out her hand, but Ada didn't seem to notice so Roxy gestured down at her apron, embarrassed. "Yes, um, I'm afraid we aren't quite, um, ready for the grand welcome we wanted to give you." What was happening to her? All Roxy's confidence and excitement had evaporated at the sight of this officious, elegant woman.

"It's fine," Ada said, though her mouth twitched. She didn't look impressed. "I will go to my room and do some editing on the mag while you," she looked Roxy up and down, "pull yourself together." Ada Okafor ran a travel magazine for rich Nigerians who wanted to jet-set around the world like she did. She had a huge international following on Instagram in the luxury travel market.

Ada looked around. "But who will carry my bags?"

CHAPTER TWO

THREE MONTHS EARLIER, the Funky Cat Inn had been a guesthouse known as Evangeline's. It was a large, grand house built in the French architecture style so common in New Orleans. But when Roxy arrived, the building had long since begun to crumble and fall into disrepair. It was covered in cobwebs. The balcony on the third floor was so rickety that no one dared step out on it. The once-vibrant pink façade had peeled and faded in patches until it was blush in one corner and almost white in another. Bookings were down, and one guest turned out to be a murderer. But then Evangeline retired, Sam infused an injection of cash, and Roxy had taken over. Now the place was transformed.

Roxy's do-over had started with the exterior. No one was going to be staying with her if the place looked like a flamingo on its last leg. She had gotten busy with a stepladder and used up can after can of bright pink paint until the first floor dazzled. She stopped there because she wasn't a fan of heights, and instead hired a professional who brought his ladder and took over. Now the outside of the building had been restored to its former brilliance. It stood out like a beacon among the black, white, yellow, and red buildings around it.

Roxy had bitten her lip as she watched the painter from the cobbled, narrow street below. Hiring someone had seemed an extravagance. To save money, she had done most of the work around the hotel herself with the help of Nat and Sam, but she knew she must recognize her limits. It would hardly help to save money on a painter if she fell off a ladder and broke her leg. But still, her poverty-stricken background and her thrifty ways made spending money on the renovations hard for her.

Sam had been a huge help. As well as being both an excellent handyman and the owner of a nearby laundry, he was also an awesome sax player, a car enthusiast, and apparently an all-round decent guy. Sam's most important role at present, however, was that he was the main investor in the hotel, both buying the building from Evangeline *and* paying for its renovations. He had given Roxy a budget, and she had made sure to keep well within it.

The form of Sam's relationship with Roxy had an unresolved quality around it, though. Roxy knew she had a crush on him, one that she was trying to quell. She suspected he was attracted to her too. Over the weeks and months of renovating the building together, they'd built a friendly, but platonic working relationship, their mutual attraction only slightly impinging upon it now and again. Neither had made a move on the other, either because they were too scared or too busy. Roxy wasn't too sure which it might be, and now she felt it best to keep things as they were. It didn't do to mix business with pleasure in her book. She didn't want to destroy a good thing. And now, as part-owner and manager of the Funky Cat, she most definitely had a good thing.

Where Sam got his money from was a second unresolved question that had caused Roxy some sleepless nights. The laundry business was doing great, sure, but the cash needed to buy the hotel? That was more than a laundry business owner could be expected to shell out. *And* he owned a Rolls Royce!

"Where does he get his money from?" Roxy had asked Nat one day.

Nat had shrugged. "He doesn't say. We don't ask." It was all a bit of a mystery.

Roxy's life gave her no time to ponder the question, however. After the Funky Cat's exterior was made over, she turned her attention to organizing the area out front in the courtyard. The hotel faced onto Elijah's Bakery. The owner, Elijah was a great friend and a wonderful baker. Daily he provided the Funky Cat with fresh bread, delicious pastries, and, of course, beignets. Elijah also played the piano and rounded out the jazz trio that performed at the Funky Cat alongside Nat and Sam.

Elijah was a snappy dresser. When he wasn't working, he was kitted out in bright shirts and gleaming, patent leather crocodile shoes. He loved a stripe pattern or an African print. But when it came to his business, his personal style didn't translate. While Elijah might have been a master baker, he was *not* a master decorator. The façade of his building looked like it hadn't been updated since the 1980s. It was entirely black and white and gray. Roxy, with some effort, had persuaded him to paint it, and he'd chosen a pale pink and mint-green color scheme. Now the two businesses that sat opposite each other were also a match for one another. The buildings were even color-coordinated.

"I can't believe I didn't do this years ago!" Elijah said to Roxy when they stood back and surveyed his storefront. A huge grin spread across his face, and he gave Roxy a high five. He bought new cast iron tables and chairs for the outside, and Sam had given him a special deal on linen tablecloths and napkins to finish off the bright, clean look. Now the bakery was doing better than ever with clientele drawn to it by its elegant, comfortable surroundings and the smell of fresh coffee and beignets that emanated from it.

Roxy and Elijah had become firm friends as they strived to build successful businesses while staying true to their values. They both believed in offering a great product at a great price with friendly service, hard work, and decency being their driving forces. They could often be found outside Elijah's bakery nursing coffees, their heads together as they discussed the finer points of running a business.

Finally, there was just one thing left to do to the outside of the Funky Cat: they needed to add the finishing touches to the courtyard. First, Sam came along with a pressure washer and took out years of encrusted grime from between the cobbles. Then it was on to the decoration. Roxy had decided to incorporate as many plants as possible into the design of the new courtyard, and her friend Sage was just the right person to help her.

Sage was a spiritualist, New Orleans born and bred, with an ancestral line of African American spiritual women stretching back behind her into history. It was in her blood. She stood in the newly cleaned courtyard in her flowing robes, a deep emerald green this particular time, stretching her hands out. "I'm letting the spirits come to me," she said. "You need to place pots around. They should be filled with basil and white sage and rosemary and lavender. Here, here, here, and here," she said to Roxy, pointing at four spots in the space in front of the hotel. "They will ward away evil spirits, and I will invite angels and other benevolent spiritual beings to bless and protect this space."

Roxy wasn't entirely sure she believed in all that, but she guessed it couldn't hurt. Besides, it would make the entrance to the Funky Cat smell wonderful. She placed huge pots of herbs just as Sage had directed and hung baskets overflowing with brightly-colored blooms from the exterior walls. Finally, Sam hung a sign with the name of the hotel emblazoned across it under a rendering of a cat that looked rather like Nefertiti, Roxy's long-haired white Persian. The cat on the sign was wearing a trilby hat at a jaunty angle and holding a saxophone.

The courtyard now looked so good that Roxy was satisfied that the standard of the outside of the hotel matched that of the inside. The interior of the building had come a *long* way in the time since Roxy had taken over and in the process of restoring it, she had uncovered yet another useful talent of Nat's—restoring or repurposing worn neglected furniture and decorations.

"It's called 'upcycling,' Rox, and you can do it with just about anything if you have the right eye and the tools," Nat had said. "Beauty on the cheap." The hotel had benefited from her passion enormously.

They'd transformed the dining room into a grand eating area and the lounge into a sumptuous, decadent sanctuary for relaxation and rest. They had furnished the rooms with a mixture of real antiques and upcycled items in a variety of dark woods, silver, and gold, with occasional touches of powdery blue. The bedrooms had had a similar treatment. But Roxy still worried that there wasn't enough color, so she and Nat went through, adding splashes of flamingo pink and royal blue and gold—a cushion here, a toothbrush holder there, until there was a heightened vibrancy to each room.

"It's so fantastic, Rox. You're gonna be on TV soon, I just know it," Nat said to her soon after they opened.

Word-of-mouth recommendations about the Funky Cat spread quickly. After her Grand Opening event, as news of Roxy's relaunch of the hotel became known, business picked up. Roxy had seen a dramatic increase in bookings and the hotel was now at full capacity nearly every night.

"Oh, I don't know about that, but it is pretty amazing, isn't it?" Roxy had felt her confidence grow in leaps as the days passed. The Roxy of old—anxious, wallflower Roxy— seemed to have gone. An energetic, confident business-woman had replaced her. Roxy was mostly fine with her transformation, but occasionally doubts emerged. She knew that despite her efforts and the professional demeanor she strived to project, there were times when she wasn't quite as together as she appeared. Now though, it was showtime. Whatever the next few days had in store for her, Roxy had a responsibility to be calm, unflappable, and in charge. The game was most definitely on.

CHAPTER THREE

NAT RETURNED TO the kitchen red-faced and scowling. "What did that woman bring with her, the entire contents of Harrods? She told me she'd just been to England and had 'stocked up on essentials.' *Essentials?* She thinks all these Burberry trench coats and designer dresses are essentials? Really!" Whenever she was angry, Nat's British accent became more pronounced, all clipped tones and short vowels. "And not only did I have to carry all those bags upstairs, but I also had to get a load of the clothes out, hang them up *and* check for damage and creases."

Roxy was surprised Nat had played along with Ada's requests. "Doesn't sound like you, Nat."

"I know." Nat flopped on one of the stools they kept in the kitchen and pushed her short dark hair back from her face. "Normally I would have told her to jog on. I mean, I'm not her personal assistant, am I? But I knew I had to do it. Imagine, what if she had been secretly filming and I told her I wasn't going to help? It wouldn't make a good impression, would it now?"

"Right," said Roxy biting her lip. She was already wondering if they had gotten themselves in too deep with this Instagram promotion. They'd had plenty of guests before, but those were nice *normal* ones. Perhaps naïvely, she'd thought the Instagram influencers would be the same. "Thanks for taking one for the team."

Nat rolled her eyes and hopped off the stool. She began to drench the bread pudding Roxy had prepared earlier with caramel and whiskey sauce. "Well, the next few days are going to be *fun, fun, fun,* aren't they?" she said, pulling a face and clapping her hands. "Just four more guests to go. Let's hope they're not all as demanding as Ada. We'll not cope."

To Roxy and Nat's relief, Ada didn't make as much work for them that afternoon as they feared. She called down to reception for soda water but stayed quiet the remainder of the time. There was a lot of work to do in the kitchen, and Roxy, Nat, and Evangeline did not need distractions.

When everything was prepared and laid out for the evening meal, Roxy hurried to shower and change. Since transforming the hotel, she'd had part of a downstairs storage area turned into two rooms—a bedroom and a bathroom. These were now her private quarters. The room at the top of the house where she'd first stayed as a visitor had been transformed into a wonderful penthouse-style suite. That's where they were going to put Lily Vashchenko, one of the other influencers. She had the most followers, but now Roxy wondered if she should have put Ada Okafor in there.

Roxy went into her room and slipped off her shoes. She padded in her socks over to the bed where her fluffy white princess of a cat Nefertiti was curled up, purring away. Roxy tickled her under her chin. "Hello, my love," she said. "You look so cozy there."

Nefertiti looked up at her, gave a little mewl in appreciation and closed her eyes in what appeared to be ecstasy as Roxy rubbed her cheek.

There was nothing Roxy loved more than curling up with a good book and Nefertiti on her lap. But there was little time for that these days, what with all the hotel work going on, and there was absolutely no time for it now! She took a lightning-fast shower and slipped into a crisp, pressed, white shirt, tight jeans, and silver pumps. She heard a knock on the front door and quickly looked in the mirror before smoothing her hair.

As she came out of her room she was immediately faced two young men in T-shirts, jeans, and hoodies. Unlike Ada, they had their cameras at the ready.

"So we've just arrived at the Funky Cat," one of the men was saying. Roxy recognized him as Michael O'Sullivan. He had dark hair, thin lips, and a serious-looking face. "Isn't it looking grand?"

The other man jumped in front of the camera, pulling a silly face. "Woohoo! Far too grand for the likes of me!" Roxy knew he was Dash Davies, recognizing him from his unruly red hair, wild grin, and bright T-shirt. He was known for always wearing some wild color or other. Together the two men made up the Instagram and YouTube star duo *Michael & Dash*. They toured the world in a variety of styles, from budget to luxury, and while Michael compiled the serious reviews, Dash always had a trick up his sleeve to make things interesting and, Roxy suspected, boost views. He posted videos with such titles as *The Ice Bucket Challenge . . . In Greenland!* Or *Man Downs 100 Pints of Lager in London!*

"Hey there!" Roxy said with a huge smile. Her heart was pounding. She knew she was on camera, and despite the position she was now in, she still wasn't at all used to fame, notoriety, or even people noticing her. She'd only recently allowed Sage to include pictures of her on their own Funky Cat Instagram profile. "The stars of *Michael & Dash*! So glad to have you guys here! My name's Roxy, I'm part-owner and manager of this hotel. I'll be your host during your time with us."

Dash bounded forward and wrapped her up in a hug. "We're totally pumped to be here!" he said into her shoulder, a little too loud for comfort. Then he backed up. "Me and Mike have been . . ."

"*Michael*," his partner said.

"Oh sorry, I forgot." Dash slapped his hand to his forehead. He looked at Roxy and grinned. "I do have a tendency to be overly familiar. Excuse me. *Michael*." He gave a little bow and discreetly rolled his eyes at Roxy as he straightened up. "So, anyway, we were saying, we're so totally excited to come to New Orleans to get our dose of the culture. We want to eat ourselves silly on all that Creole goodness. I'm planning to put on at least ten pounds. Can you hook me up, Rox?"

Roxy laughed. "I certainly can. *And,* if you turn the camera around, you'll see someone who'll make sure of it." She pointed out the door. "That's Elijah's Bakery, and he makes the meanest beignets–they're square donuts–the world has ever seen. We stock up on them for breakfast."

"Sounds like a plan, Roxy!" said Dash. Then he grabbed his case. "Right! Where's my room?"

"Come with me!" Roxy said feeling excited now. While Michael was quiet and serious—maybe a little pompous—Dash's energy was contagious.

But they didn't get very far. Before they'd ascended four steps, there was a cheery "Hello!" at the door.

CHAPTER FOUR

ROXY TURNED TO see an older woman in her late 60s, her gray hair cropped short, rather like Roxy's. She wore a big smile and an equally large backpack. Compared to Roxy's earlier guests, she cut a quiet, modest figure. She was dressed in cargo pants, a plain gray T-shirt, and hiking boots. In her hand, she carried two trekking poles. For one horrifying moment, Roxy couldn't remember her name before it came rushing back to her. "Sylvia Walters!" She was a travel influencer from Maine. Most of her followers were women aged 65 and over.

Sylvia had obviously done her research. "You must be Roxy Reinhardt."

"Indeed I am." Roxy came down the steps and shook her hand. "I can show you all up to your rooms. We're ready for you."

"No personalized service?" Michael muttered. He spoke softly, but loud enough for Roxy to hear. Everyone went quiet.

"Michael!" Dash hissed, giving him a little shove on his shoulder.

Unfortunately, the shove was a little *too* hard, and Michael fell down the four steps they'd just climbed. The camera crashed to the ground, and Michael stumbled, then over-corrected, finally splaying out at the bottom of the stairs.

"Ow!" he said.

Roxy and Sylvia gasped. Dash hurried down the stairs. "Oh my gosh! I'm so sorry! I didn't mean to . . ."

"Shut up!" Michael said, pushing him away roughly. "You could have seriously hurt me."

"Are you okay?" Roxy asked, peering at him.

"Who cares about me?" Michael barked, reaching out for the camera that had crashed to the ground when he fell. "It's this I'm worried about." He took a look and nodded. "Thank goodness. Still intact and still recording." He turned the camera back to himself. "Well, I just took a dive, but I'm fine now. See you guys in a little while." He pressed a button and the red recording light flicked off. "Hmph. Let's carry on."

Dash looked embarrassed. "I'm real sorry, bud."

"I wouldn't worry about it too much," said Sylvia. "Drama always commands attention. You might even become a meme!"

Roxy saw Michael's facial expression darken, and she jumped in quickly before the conversation turned into an argument. "Let's get you up to your rooms, everybody!"

Roxy, having felt excited just a few minutes earlier, was feeling stressed now and wondered again if this Instagram promotion had been such a great idea after all. She tried to hide her fears with a smile. Dash seemed to read her thoughts because as they turned the corner on the staircase, he patted her on the shoulder. "Don't worry, Roxy. We're not litigious."

Roxy laughed nervously. "Well, that's something." She hadn't even *thought* of that. She settled her guests into their rooms without further fuss, but by the time she returned downstairs, she felt a little sick. What *had* she let herself in for? She popped her head in the kitchen to see how things were progressing. Nat was hard at work at the counter while Evangeline was flitting between pans like a fly.

"How's progress?" Roxy asked. She paused. "Nat, don't you need to get dressed?"

Nat stuck her tongue out. "We have it all under control, thank you. Anyway, I'm just booting it, so no rush." Roxy knew what she meant. Nat was *not* a dressing-up sort of girl. She loved her black distressed jeans and band tees and big combat boots. Roxy doubted even a million dollars could get her slipping into something slinky. When it came to dinnertime, Nat usually just changed her shoes, from the worn-down boots she wore every day to something a little fancier.

Nat had amassed quite a collection of Doc Martens over the months of working at the Funky Cat—purple sparkly ones, teal patent ones, silver-and-black stripy ones, and a black patent pair with red ribbon laces that tied in a huge bow. Each time she got a paycheck, she put some aside for her next purchase. The boots, while not elegant, were part of Nat. They gave her character. She also put a brush through her short, unruly hair, which transformed it into a pretty, sleek bob. Her tattoo sleeves still showed, though. All in all, Roxy had reconciled herself to Nat's appearance and just about considered her trademark look an asset, a nod to the quirky character of the Funky Cat *Inn*. She certainly sparked conversation between the guests at mealtimes.

Despite Nat's tongue poke, Roxy smiled back at her and said, "It's smelling delicious. I can't wait!" She looked around at the food preparations laid out in the kitchen. It gave her butterflies to know that much of the next few days would be memorialized in perpetuity in videos and pictures and reviews. Were they really ready? She shook her head. It was too late to think about that. At least she could rely on the food not to let her down.

Her nerves made her want to start fixing everything. She headed back into the dining room where Nat had laid out fancy white tablecloths and huge place settings with reams of cutlery for each person. Three vases of flowers graced the center of the table. Roxy clasped her hands and tapped them against her mouth as she walked around inspecting everything. She scanned every place setting, making sure each knife, fork, and spoon was just so. She tweaked the positions of the flowers. When she couldn't improve things any further, she went over to the lounge area and checked that all the cushions—blue and bronze—were in perfect alignment.

"Hello?" a deep female voice called out from the hallway.

Roxy hurried through to the entrance. "Hello, there!" she said. The final influencer to arrive, Lily Vashchenko, was in front of her. Lily was tall, much taller than Roxy, and older, perhaps in her early thirties. Waves of blonde that emerged from darker roots bounced over her shoulders. She had slanted almond eyes that were distinctly Slavic and made her look innocent but a little seductive at the same time. She wore tight white jeans and a white swishy top with silver butterflies fluttering all over it. Black stilettos with a silver heel finished off her ensemble along with big silver jewelry that pierced her ears and lay around her neck.

"You must be Roxy," Lily said somberly. She placed her palms on Roxy's shoulders and bent in to air kiss her on both cheeks. Roxy, her mouth forming a perfect "O," couldn't help but allow herself to be embraced like this. "Lovely to meet you, Lily." As Lily let her hands fall, Roxy watched Lily's rose gold iPhone warily—was she filming?

Lily saw her glance and said smoothly, "I'm not recording yet. That would be bad manners. You're new to this whole business, so I shall not put any pressure on you. I'm only going to put good things in this review, don't worry." Lily had a thick Russian accent. She grabbed the handle of her large suitcase, also rose-gold, and smiled, cat-like, the skin around her eyes creasing at the corners. "So, where's my room?" Lily tilted her head to one side and smiled with her lips pressed together. "I don't know you, but I am proud of you for running such a lovely hotel. That's such an achievement at your age."

"Thank you! Please come with me," Roxy said, unsure whether to be flattered or patronized, but she was glad to be able to tell Lily, "You're getting the penthouse suite!"

CHAPTER FIVE

A T 6 PM, ROXY called up to the guests' rooms to let them know that dinner would be served in an hour. She told them that beforehand they could relax in the lounge and have the nibbles she'd prepared: chips, pistachio and cashew nuts, olives, and champagne. Then they'd head to the huge dining table for their meal.

In preparation for the evening, Roxy changed into a purple satin dress and paired it with silver sparkling shoes and a silver necklace and earrings. Before Roxy arrived in New Orleans, she'd loved clothes and jewelry, but never had the confidence to wear show-stopping outfits. She felt like a kid playing dress-up when she tried. She also hadn't had the budget for anything but basics. She'd stuck mostly with jeans, plain skirts, sweaters, and tees. But now? Now, she had a newfound confidence and she was making the most of it! Nat had shown her the best thrift stores in the city, and Roxy had become an exceptional bargain hunter, kitting out her wardrobe with the kind of outfits that befitted her role at the hotel but on a very small budget.

There was nothing else for it in her opinion, New Orleans and her position simply demanded glitz and glamor.

Roxy didn't have time to do anything special with her hair, not that there was a lot she could do with it—it was a pixie cut after all—so she simply finger-combed it, and with a flick of mascara and a slick of lip gloss, she was ready to go.

Roxy had laid out glasses on a tray on top of one of the coffee tables, a couple of bottles of champagne resting in ice coolers beside it. After calling her guests, she had hovered, ready to greet them with a glass of bubbly, conscious that each and every moment was a video and review opportunity. She didn't want to give the influencers the slightest chance to produce anything negative.

While Roxy waited, she wondered if they had *already* made any less than favorable content for their Instagram accounts. She had an overwhelming temptation to whip out her own phone and check, but she resisted. It wouldn't look very professional if the influencers sauntered in ready for the finest New Orleans had to offer and found her glued to her phone like a teenager so it stayed in her little glittery cross-body bag, firmly on silent.

Sam arrived first. He brought his saxophone with him and looked suave and sophisticated in a gray tux. "Hi, Rox," he said, setting his sax at the back of the room behind one of the luxurious couches. "Everything ready?" His eyes were lit up with excitement on Roxy's behalf.

"I hope so!" Roxy said. "I'm a bit nervous. Their arrival wasn't entirely without a hitch, but I think the meal will go well."

"You'll be absolutely fine. You'll do great, in fact. You've worked so hard on this place and . . ."

"With *your* help," Roxy interrupted. She knew she'd

landed on her feet thanks to Sam and Evangeline and felt a little guilty about it, though she didn't quite know why.

"It's been an absolute privilege to help," Sam said firmly in his lovely low voice. "I didn't want to see this place turned over to a developer, torn down, and turned into shiny new apartments any more than you did. This is my heritage. Yours now too."

"I know," Roxy said. "But thank you all the same."

"You're welcome. Now I won't hear any more about it," he said briskly. He bent over the ice bucket containing the champagne. "May I pour you a glass, Ms. Luxury Hotel Manager?"

Roxy laughed. "Please do. Though I won't have much, or I'll be spilling my secrets to the world via Instagram video."

"Ha!" Sam said. "The deep dark secrets of Roxy Reinhardt. Are you part of a criminal underworld?"

"Busted," Roxy said with a smile, taking the glass of champagne from him. "Don't blow my cover now. Or I'll have you . . ." She raised her eyebrows, and her glass, in a meaningful way, "dealt with."

"Ooh hoo!" Sam said. "That's me told." They stared at one another over their champagne for just a little longer than necessary before a door closing behind them eased the tension.

Sage and Elijah had arrived. Sage, as ever, looked like something from another world. She'd dusted her cheekbones with silver glitter that shimmered in the lamplight, and she had a wreath of silver and deep pink flowers on her head. Magenta robes flowed loosely around her frame and brushed the ground. Silver sandals peeked out from beneath.

"Looking like a dream as always!" Roxy said to her, giving Sage a kiss on the cheek.

Sage gave a humble little bow and said, "May the golden light of blessings engulf you." Being engulfed, even with blessings, seemed rather overwhelming to Roxy, but she was quite certain Sage's intentions were kind.

With Sage came Elijah. He strode into the hotel in a dark purple suit and bright white shiny shoes with gold flecks. A black shirt with a gold bow tie completed his look. His reputation for flamboyant outfits wouldn't suffer that night.

"Hey, hey, hey, it's crunch time!" Elijah said, which didn't help to calm Roxy's nerves in the least. "Time to let the Funky Cat spread its wings and fly!"

"Cats fly now, do they?" Sam said.

"In some mediums," said Sage, gravely. She was a vegetarian and loved animals. Her expertise in the spiritual realm gave her an otherworldly view of them. "On the human plane, cats' wings are clipped." She put her hand to her chest like she was in pain, feeling the cruelty toward the felines in her own heart. "But they do fly. In the astral sphere, they are free."

The others stared back at her astonished as she looked at them seriously before bursting into giggles, clutching her chest.

"You should see your faces!" she said. "I'm kidding! Well, mostly." She winked at them.

"I don't know when you're kidding or serious, darling," Elijah said to her. "It's all weird and fantastic to me." He turned to Roxy, kissing her on both cheeks. "Did you get those pastries I sent over? They are specially for the influencers."

"Yep, I guessed."

Elijah had made custom cupcakes for each of the guests. Each one was decorated with the Instagram logo and the guest's name. "They look fantastic and adorable, Elijah. Thank you. Nat will deliver them to the guests' rooms along with a personalized thermos of brandy milk punch while they're eating so it's a nice surprise for them after their meal, like a sort of nightcap."

"Marvelous. You think of the finest of touches, girl-friend," Elijah said.

Before long, Roxy's important guests trickled in. Michael and Dash didn't really *do* the whole tux thing, but they came down in linen suits and snappy dark brown leather shoes. Ada, the Nigerian socialite, was absolutely stunning in a long white gown that made her skin look richer than ever. It hugged her slim body, and she looked like a million bucks. Sylvia, the influencer from Maine, looked smart in a navy blue pantsuit and Mary Janes, while Lily, the tall, slightly haughty influencer who was staying in the penthouse suite, wore a little cocktail dress in pink. It was her favorite color. Her Instagram profile was awash with it.

Roxy had decided that all her friends would sit down to dinner with the influencers, just as they often did with her guests. This mingling of friends and visitors had been a part of the tradition of the hotel when it was *Evangeline's*. It created a warm, homey atmosphere. Elijah was always on hand with a joke, and Sam could be relied on to charm the guests and provide great conversation. Sage exuded good-will toward others and might read their fortunes, while Nat could be great fun under the right circumstances. She had been known to burst into glorious song after dinner and would take requests if she was in a particularly good mood. It was true that Evangeline wasn't the most sociable of people, she certainly wasn't a party animal or a social butterfly, but she could talk at length about New Orleans and would introduce the guests to all sorts of hidden attractions they would not have otherwise discovered. Roxy, of course, would be the consummate host.

CHAPTER SIX

A FTER CHAMPAGNE, THE influencers, Roxy, and her friends sat down at the table. Roxy had suggested offering canapés, but Evangeline had said she wasn't a fan of all that "newfangled, posh fiddly stuff." She preferred serving a good, hearty New Orleans dinner that didn't come with any fussy, fancy crudités or appetizers. Instead, the meal began with gumbo.

Normally Evangeline would have made it thick and filling, but since they were having so many courses, they had decided a lighter version would be more appropriate. Naturally, the influencers got out their phones and began to snap pictures before they tucked in. Lily Vashchenko even arranged the napkin and cutlery in a delicate arrangement next to her bowl and angled the picture so that she got some of the lounge décor in the frame. Roxy was sure it would look impressive and made a mental note to check the post on Instagram later.

After the flurry of clicking and updating of statuses had been completed, the influencers settled down to eat, all of them seeming to enjoy the gumbo a great deal. They made the right noises, even Ada, and they all complimented Evangeline. After that, they moved on to the crawfish and cheese pie course where the frenzy of picture composition and status updating started all over again.

Roxy watched them, fascinated, and wondered how animated and raucous the night was going to get. Dash, in particular, seemed to be enjoying himself. There was plenty of wine on the table, and she noticed how he repeatedly filled up his glass with one of the reds from a local Louisiana winery.

"You really should drink white wine, you know," Ada said, sniffing, "since we're having so much fish."

"Meh," Dash said with a shrug. "I don't really like white, to be honest. I'm more of a red-blooded man," he winked, "if you know what I mean." Ada looked down her nose at him.

"You go ahead with your red," Sylvia said kindly, then chuckled. "Live on the wild side!" She had barely touched her glass of white, and her champagne flute from earlier sat next to it, still half full.

"Wine messes with my palate." Ada sipped her water with pursed lips. "I wouldn't drink such cheap wine anyway." At that, Roxy had to hold her tongue. It wasn't a cheap wine! She'd taken a deep breath and splurged out on bottles that cost over $100 each. They were drinking some of the best wine produced in Louisiana. But Roxy guessed Ada was used to everything being high-end luxury. Roxy had heard Ada mention her father's private jet as she chatted to Lily when they were drinking their champagne before the meal.

Roxy had grown up with her single mother in a poor, rural area in Ohio. She had never met her father. She didn't even know his name. So while drinking $100 bottles of wine in a boutique hotel might be a step down for Ada, it was an entire staircase *up* for Roxy, a life which, when she was younger, she never imagined living. People in the neighborhood where she was raised were doing well if they had a steady job, even if it was bagging at the local grocery store for minimum wage. As long as they could buy their own food and they had roofs over their heads, even if it was a trailer roof, they were relieved if not exactly content. Roxy imagined Ada walking through her old neighborhood, sniffing at the trailers and the children who played outside, some of whom had holes in their shoes. Their separate experiences of the world were completely different. But that didn't matter now. Roxy was aware of her responsibility to her guests, her staff, and the wider community. They all depended upon the Funky Cat being a success. Roxy shook her head to bring herself back to the present.

Next came the main course, Shrimp Creole with rice and jalapeño cornbread. It was Roxy's absolute favorite. Lily Vashchenko languidly snapped pictures of the "cute little ramekins," taking a flower from one of the vases on the table to place it in her picture while everyone raved about the shrimp.

"Fabulous food, Nat, Roxy!" Sylvia said.

Even though Evangeline had done most of the work, the elderly woman kept quiet with a secret smile on her face, knowing that she was passing the glory of Creole and Cajun cooking onto the next generation. Roxy was extremely proud and glad that she was keeping this grand old tradition alive and was inordinately grateful to Evangeline for taking the time to teach them her recipes.

"Credit where it's due. This is all thanks to Evangeline," Nat said modestly.

Dash paused, his fork loaded. "Evangeline is a lovely name," he said. "Where does it come from?"

"It's Greek, right?" Michael began before Evangeline could even open her mouth.

Evangeline winked and said, "You're right about that, cher. You've done your research. It means 'bearer of good news' so your luck might be in." She looked at Dash and smiled. "Your name's not that common. What does it mean? Apart from the obvious, of course."

"It's short for Dashiell," he said. "It's Scottish. Apparently, my ancestors came from the highest Highlands of Scotland, which probably means they were raving mad murderous warriors back in the thirteenth century or something. The name doesn't mean anything as far as I am aware, at least nothing exciting."

Nat laughed. "It does suit you, though! You're always dashing around the place. You're going to India one day, Canada the next! You dash all around the world. I'd love to do that!"

Dash leaned forward, his eyes bright with excitement. "So why don't you?" he said in an encouraging voice. "I love experiencing different cultures, different types of people. And when I make a load more money from this Instagram and YouTube business, I want to *help people*. Build schools and hospitals. I can't wait!" He breathed out, his eyes gleaming with visions of his dreams. "I think you should travel the world, Nat. It would give you a totally new perspective."

Nat looked a little awkward and mumbled something about New Orleans feeling like home before dashing from the table to serve dessert.

"This is a lot of food," Lily said, exhaling discreetly through full, pouting lips. "I can barely take another bite."

Lily had only been nibbling at her food, a bite here, a taste there. Roxy supposed that was how she maintained her lithe figure.

"It's certainly very filling," Michael agreed, as Dash snapped away, taking a picture of the warm bread pudding soaked with caramel and whiskey. Soft, slightly melted vanilla ice cream made waves through the brown sauce making it look delicious and lush. It smelled heavenly, and Roxy knew from experience it tasted even better.

Nevertheless, after the snapping and posing and updating and submitting was over, they all, perhaps with the exception of Lily, fell on the pudding, silence pervading the room as they focused on the delicious dessert.

"Mmmm, this is slipping down a treat," Sylvia said.

"We have cheese next," Nat reminded them.

Michael took the camera from Dash and pointed it at him.

"Cheese? This is CRAZY," Dash said into the camera. "Five courses . . . five! That's how you know this is a real luxury place. You know, the local wine is really great too." He raised his wine glass a little wildly and then lowered it to take a sip as he leaned into the camera. But as he did so, he knocked his chin against the glass.

"Dash!" Michael said, but it was too late. The damage was done. Dash's red wine had launched itself all over Ada Okafor's pristine white gown.

CHAPTER SEVEN

"OH, MY GOODNESS!" Ada shrieked, jumping to her feet. The front of her white dress was stained with so much red wine it looked like she'd been stabbed.

"Oh, oh, oh," Roxy said, rushing over to her.

"Noooooo!" Dash said, his eyes bulging with horror. "I'm so, so sorry, Ada!"

Elijah leaned over. "Never fear, Elijah is here." He started patting the stain with his napkin.

"Get your hands off me!" Ada screamed. Elijah snapped his hand back like a slapped child.

Sage didn't make a move, but closed her eyes and placed her hands, palms upwards, her fingertips touching. She was an oasis of calm in an uproarious sea.

"Dash! You fool!" said Michael. He was still recording.

Evangeline, shaking her head like a disapproving grand-mother, put her arm around Ada. "Come on, cher, no real harm done, let's get you cleaned up."

But Ada wriggled away. "You get *off* of me too!" She

radiated fury. "How dare you! This is *a Versace!*" she shouted at Dash. "Do you know who I am? My father . . ."

"Sorry to interrupt!" Sam hollered over her. "But trust me, you need to act fast on that stain. I'm a laundry guy, and I know what I'm talking about." They all swiveled their horrified gazes from Ada to Sam. "You'll have to take your dress off and pour white wine over it fast. I'll run to the laundry and get some proper stain remover. We can save your dress, but only if we move very quickly." Sam dashed to the door and disappeared.

"Finally, someone who speaks sense," Ada said, recovering some of her composure. She stood and began to strip down to her underwear in the middle of the dining room.

Roxy's eyes widened. "Let me get you a robe!" she called over and rushed to her bedroom to fetch one.

Dash still looked horrified at what he'd done. He leaned back in his chair, his hands clasped across the top of his head. His partner, Michael, was deadpan as he recorded surreptitiously, the camera resting on the table, the shining red "record" button the only sign that it was on.

When Roxy hurried back, Nat, her eyes transfixed by the sight of Ada standing in the middle of the dining room in her underwear, was pressing her lips together so tightly they were white. Her throat was bobbing up and down. She was clearly trying not to laugh.

"Oh, so it's funny, is it?" Ada said to Nat.

"The Universe has its little jokes with us sometimes, in this realm of chaos," Sage said. Her low, soft voice could make any words sound soothing, but Ada looked at her like she had two heads.

Roxy offered her robe to the Nigerian woman who immediately swiped it from her, handing Roxy her red-stained dress in exchange. Roxy took it and glared at Nat,

"Come with me into the kitchen to fix this up." Nat didn't respond immediately. "Nat!"

But Nat didn't move fast enough, so Roxy grabbed her by the wrist, pulling her into the kitchen. She shut the door behind them. "What are you playing at?" she hissed while finding some white wine to douse the dress with. "Don't you know this is all going on the internet? This could ruin us! Why are you grinning?"

"What?" said Nat, smiling. Roxy couldn't remember the last time she felt so angry. Then Nat sighed. "Oh . . . okay, I see what you mean. Sorry, it was just a teentsy-weentsy bit funny. She just stood in the mid . . ." Nat looked like she was about to burst into a fit of giggles again.

"Stop it! You're jeopardizing everything!" Roxy hissed, still furious, and, if she were honest, scared to death at what this debacle might mean for her business. "It's bad enough that this has happened, but you're staff! You can't laugh at her!"

"I didn't actually laugh!" Nat protested.

"Near enough. Look, pull yourself together. I know you don't like her, but still."

Nat stifled her giggles, "You're right. I'm sorry. How can I help?"

Just then, Ada burst through the kitchen door. She was quite a sight. Her eyes were wild and her shiny high heels and Roxy's robe made an unconventional fashion statement. "How's it going?" she growled, her arms outstretched, her hands curled like claws in front of her. She dropped them the moment she noticed Nat, folded her arms and pursed her lips. "Not that *you* care."

"I'll just go clean the wine from the floor," Nat mumbled. She left the kitchen, avoiding Ada's withering look.

"I think your dress is doing okay so far," Roxy said to Ada. The white wine was spreading over the red stain and seemed to be neutralizing it. There was still some discoloration though, a light pink. "I just hope Sam comes back quickly."

"He'd better," Ada said. "I don't know what you're thinking, bringing that Dash prankster person here. Who does he think he is? You need to ask him to leave. In fact, my whole visit here has been a poor one. No one to greet me, no personal service. Are you sure you know what you're doing?"

A lump formed in Roxy's throat while butterflies chaotically danced in her belly. At that moment she felt she *was* in over her head, just like she'd feared in her least confident moments. And now she was in a bind. If she asked Dash to leave per Ada's request, surely it would be some huge scandal that Michael & Dash would milk for all they were worth, probably for months, on their social media accounts. It might ruin her business. But if she let him stay, what would Ada do? Ada had huge influence among affluent tourists—especially in the African and Middle Eastern markets. They were the type of clients who desired luxury experiences and Roxy was quite sure Ada had the power to generate a negative buzz. Perhaps they would all turn on her and destroy everything she'd worked for. She blew out her cheeks. At least it would be over quickly.

She didn't know what to say to Ada. She was in a no-win situation. So she smiled brightly. "Let's hope Sam hurries up; we need to save this dress!" she said. "It must have cost a ton."

"It's not about the cost. It's *never* about the cost," Ada snapped. She even stamped her foot on the tiled kitchen floor. "This is a Versace *limited edition*."

CHAPTER EIGHT

"**O**H," ROXY SAID. She didn't even know it was possible to have a limited edition Versace dress. She looked up to the ceiling and down to the floor. Her thoughts started to run, and they followed a familiar theme. Had there been a time in her life when she felt more inadequate? Her owning and running a business had happened so quickly. It had skyrocketed out of nowhere, in fact. And now she wondered how she'd gotten here. It had been too easy. She didn't deserve it. Evangeline and Sam must have made a mistake. The *universe* had made a mistake, surely. And now it was self-correcting. Good things like running the Funky Cat didn't happen to people like her.

"When is that big buffoon going to return?" Ada said impatiently, her eyebrows knitted together, her eyes cold and hard.

"He's *not* a buffoon," Roxy shot back without thinking. "He's a very kind, capable, strong man, and one of our dearest friends." Ada's expression didn't change.

"*And* he drives a Rolls Royce Phantom." Roxy didn't

particularly care about that, but she knew Ada would. It wasn't her finest moment, but she hated to hear Ada talk badly and without reason about Sam. It made her feel a little better to defend him.

"Really?" Ada said, perking up before relaxing and looking nonchalant. "I rode around in one before I was five. It was my father's driver's favorite car in our fleet."

"Sam's is a limited edition with maroon paint. So, you see, you two have something in common—limited editions."

"Oh." Ada nodded. "Well, that sounds nice." She offered Roxy a small smile.

Roxy smiled back, bemused at how something so inconsequential to her made such a difference to Ada. "Oh, look," she said, pointing at the dress, "it's looking pretty good now."

Ada ran her perfectly-manicured hands over the surface. "I can still see some staining."

Sam came through the door then, panting, clutching a stain-remover pen and a spray can. "I've got what I need. Let's get this fixed."

There was a rapt silence as the two women watched him work. They both looked on intently. For obvious but different reasons, Roxy and Ada *really* wanted the stain remover to work and as if by magic, it did. After a few minutes of application, the stain completely disappeared.

Ada burst into a grin and threw her arms around Sam's neck. "Oh, thank you! You are the only decent person here!"

Roxy felt an unexpected pang of jealousy course through her, closely followed by anger laced with relief. Heat rushed to her cheeks. When she'd taken on the Funky Cat, she'd decided that, despite feeling *something* for Sam, she was going to keep their friendship strictly platonic. She didn't want to mix business with pleasure. She wanted to keep things just as they were, one big, happy Funky Cat family. But she still didn't like this over-familiarity Ada was showing Sam. It ruffled her. And she didn't appreciate her comment about him being the sole arbiter of decency. They were *all* bending over backward to help *her* if only she'd notice.

Sam gave Ada an awkward pat on the back and extricated himself from her hug. "You're welcome."

"So," Ada said, smiling up at him. "I hear you have a limited edition Rolls Royce Phantom?"

"Oh, that?" he said quickly. "That's just my guilty pleasure. Shall we go back into the dining room and finish our meal?"

"So what do you do?" Ada asked, taking his arm and leaning into him. "It's so good to finally meet someone of my standing here. I'm medically trained, at Oxford University in England, but I don't practice. My father persuaded me that I was more suited for the limelight."

"Oh, right," Sam said. He sounded genuinely interested. "I took the opposite route. I studied business at Stanford. My dad wanted me to become an investment banker in New York, but I preferred the idea of a lower profile life and came back here, my home town, to start my laundry business."

Ada laughed. "And the rest. A hometown boy with a Rolls Royce? My, what did you do? Rob a bank?"

Sam laughed and got that awkward look he always did when the subject of his money came up. "Absolutely! Don't hand me in, now, Ms. Okafor!" He clapped his hands and looked at Roxy. "Right! What's next on the menu?"

Roxy's head was all awhirl, what with the red wine mishap, the complicated emotions that she was trying not to feel, *and* the new information about Sam she was learning. "Um . . ."

Evangeline rescued her by coming into the kitchen. "Time for the cheese course now," she said. "Come on, Nat."

Nat came in after her. She wouldn't make eye contact with Roxy or Ada. As Evangeline, carrying the cheese boards, followed Sam, Roxy, and Ada back out into the dining room, Nat took Elijah's personalized cupcakes from the fridge and quietly began to boil some milk.

After the cheese course, they had planned for music with Nat singing, Elijah on the piano, and Sam playing sax. Sage had offered to do tarot readings. But Roxy's energy was waning, as was everyone's, it seemed, worn out by the drama of earlier. Ada was still in her robe, her dress forgotten as she focused on Sam.

"Let's do jazz and spirits another night," Evangeline suggested. "There's always time for music and magic in New Orleans."

There was a murmur of agreement and everyone dispersed for the night. After checking that everything was locked up and safe, Roxy went to her room. She changed quickly and snuggled up with Nefertiti. The day had been overwhelming.

"Oh, Nef-nef," she said quietly into her kitty's velvety ears. "Can I really do this properly? I was just beginning to believe that I could. Is everything just going to fall apart like it always does?"

Nefertiti looked up at her and purred. Roxy shook her head sadly. "You're just a cat. You don't even care, do you? As long as I feed you and stroke you, that's all you're concerned about." Roxy looked into the cat's deep blue eyes and at her squashed-up little nose. She felt a wave of shame wash over her. She was being mean to her cat. Roxy hugged Nefertiti to her even closer. "Sorry, Nef. I just don't know what's up and what's down right now." Roxy sighed and closed her eyes. She soon slipped into a deep sleep and dreamed of dancing wine glasses and disembodied white dresses that swooped around her like ghosts at a disco.

CHAPTER NINE

"GOOD MORNING, NEFFI!" Roxy stretched her arms over her head. She felt a lot better. She had woken early and taken a long, hot shower, scrubbing away the dress drama of the night before. She did not look at Instagram to see how the incident had been portrayed there, preferring to think good thoughts and hope that everything would turn out okay in the end.

Roxy knew that even if dinner had been overshadowed by events, at least breakfast was likely to be sedate and special in real New Orleans style. They'd have beignets, of course, and café au lait and Evangeline had promised calas and couche-couche too. Calas were a type of deep-fried dumpling made from rice, egg, flour, and sugar. They were so tasty that Roxy dared not eat even one. She knew from experience that if she did, she'd scoff the whole plate. Couche-couche was Evangeline's favorite. It was made of fried cornmeal and eggs, milk, raisins, tons of syrup, often a dash of liquor too. Roxy imagined all the beautifully curated Instagram pics of the influencers' breakfasts beaming out to their followers across the world. She smiled to herself.

"Oh my gosh! Have you seen Instagram?" Nat cried out as soon as Roxy burst into the kitchen.

"No, why? What's going on?" Roxy's heart started to beat fast.

"It's gone viral!" said Nat.

"What?" Evangeline said from her place in front of the pot. "Them people have a virus? And I breathed the same air as them last night?" She wrinkled her nose and pursed her lips.

"Evangeline, you *know* what it means, I've told you before. Sage told you too. It means something's spreading fast online, just *like* a virus." Nat was abrupt.

Evangeline shook her head. "Whatever you say, cher. It's all too much for an ol' chick like me."

"It wouldn't be if you just *applied* yourself," Nat said with a sigh.

"I don't want to *apply* myself, Miss Natalie," Evangeline said, a little testy now. "I'm fine just as I am, thank you very much."

Nat rolled her eyes and turned back to Roxy. "Anyway, you know, Dash spilling wine over Ada. I mean, it *had* to go viral! They're some of the biggest influencers online, and they're having a spat! The fans are going *crazy* about it. Ada's fans are messaging Michael and Dash, threatening them with legal action and all sorts!"

"Wow," said Roxy, unsure what to think and a little confused before a feeling of dread spread over her. It was like being draped in a wet coat. Nat, on the other hand, judging by her bright eyes and excited voice, made it sound like a good thing. "I mean, I thought there would be more death threats," she continued, "but Ada's crowd are the type that sends the lawyer over to deal with their problems."

"What are Michael and Dash's fans saying?" Roxy asked. She was starting to tremble.

Nat was looking at her phone, scrolling through comments. "Some of them are saying that it was an accident while others think it was done on purpose. Even more think it's hilarious. And in all honesty, I'm inclined to agree!"

Roxy felt the anger of the night before resurfacing. "Are you crazy, Nat? Don't you realize how serious this all is?"

Nat shrugged, still looking down at her screen. "What is with you? Why do you always take life so seriously? This is great! We're getting so much publicity! And you know what they say about publicity."

"I don't want *negative* publicity," Roxy said carefully, keeping her voice even. "I want to earn a professional reputation. And right now, that is not happening."

"Professional?" Nat said. "You invited Michael and Dash for goodness sake. Didn't you know things would get wild?"

Roxy had let Sage take care of setting up the influencer campaign and had taken only a cursory look at each profile before agreeing. Now, she berated herself for not paying more attention and thinking through the implications of the campaign more carefully. At the time she'd been swept up in the excitement of the idea.

"I didn't expect it to be this wild, and even so," Roxy said, "*you* need to stay professional and not be disrespectful about the guests behind their backs, or in front of them for that matter. You've made an enemy of Ada."

"Good, because I don't like her either." Nat folded her arms, thrust out her chin and tapped her foot in defiance.

"Nat, please! You're acting like a child. Come on, Evangeline, back me up!"

"Leave me out of it!" said Evangeline. "I don't work

here anymore, and I certainly don't fix workplace arguments. I'm just a hired cook, that's all, cher. But aside from that, Nat, you should listen to your boss. You're bein' insubordinate, and she's talkin' truth."

Nat shook her head as she scrolled through the influencers' posts once more and sighed. "I suppose you're right. Roxy, I'm sorry. I will be extra nice to Ada at breakfast, I promise."

Roxy's thoughts wandered for a moment. She found herself thinking again about how ill-qualified she was to run a hotel and on top of that, now she was arguing with her staff. What kind of employer did that make her?

CHAPTER TEN

CATCHING HERSELF, ROXY quickly put all her negative thoughts to one side and decided to focus on what had to be done. It would be no good for her to be angry when the guests came downstairs. She wanted to be sunny and welcoming and represent the warmth and hospitality of New Orleans. Nausea, though, churned in her stomach. The influencer campaign was starting to become something of a disaster.

At that moment, Elijah walked in. He flounced through the swinging kitchen door holding a big white box aloft in one hand as he always did. He was delivering the first batch of pastries of the day. They would be still warm from the oven. "Here we are, my darlings. Beignets for your VIPs. Tell me, have you seen Insta this morning? My, my, those followers are *crazy*."

"Argghh, not you too, Elijah! Can't you see what this could mean for my business? We're being associated with a major social media event, a *negative* social media event. That is not the kind of publicity I had in mind when I decided to do this promotion," Roxy said.

Elijah had the decency to look abashed. "Yes, you're right," he said, more gently than she'd ever heard him. "I wouldn't like it if it were my business caught in the eye of this particular storm. It'll all blow over though, I'm sure." Elijah kissed the back of her head as he left to return to his bakery across the alleyway.

Straightening her shoulders but feeling rather abandoned and alone, Roxy took out the beignets in Elijah's box and silently arranged them in pyramids on serving platters. She took them through to the dining area and placed them on the serving table. In the empty room, Roxy checked that the coffee machine was switched on and ready, and she got out the brandy and milk and some whipping cream so her guests could garnish their coffee in true Creole style. As she looked up, she saw Ada coming down the stairs.

Ada wore a floating sundress the color of the sky and had even painted her nails to match. Roxy brought the plate of beignets over to her. "I'm so sorry about what happened last night," she said to Ada. "It was very unfortunate. How are you feeling?"

"Okay," said Ada, though she didn't sound entirely convincing. There was a hard edge to her voice, and she didn't smile. "Once you get that horrible man out of here, I will be absolutely fine. Don't worry, I won't hold you responsible for the incident. *He*, on the other hand, will be speaking to my lawyers. My father will retain the best legal team that money can buy, I can assure you of that."

"Well, I'm glad you're feeling better," Roxy said as Ada sat at the table and started to scroll through her phone. Inside, Roxy was all abuzz with nervousness. She had hoped a good night's sleep would encourage Ada to change her mind about making Dash leave. "Would you like some coffee?"

Ada didn't look up from her phone. "Actually, I'd like some of that punch we had yesterday. Please make me . . ."

Ada was interrupted by a scream and the sound of a wall being thumped. Steps pounded on the stairs and Michael rushed into the dining area. He was wild-eyed and frantic. He wore only his pajama pants. His hair was standing up on end, and for once, he carried no camera. "Quick, quick! Come quick! Somebody, anybody, quickly!" He gesticulated wildly, his voice rising with increasing frustration—no one was moving fast enough for him.

Roxy jumped away from the table and followed him as he streaked back into the hallway and up the stairs. "What's going on?" she said, feeling her breath catch in her throat.

"It's Dash! It's Dash!" Michael said. "I think . . . I think . . ." He led her into a bedroom and pointed at Dash. Michael backed into a corner of the room. He was shaking, clutching his own arms and rubbing them up and down as if it were the middle of winter, not the middle of June. It seemed to Roxy that the temperature in the room had turned icy and time had stopped. Dash was lying on his back in the bed, his skin eerily white against his red hair. "Is he . . . Is he . . . Is he . . .?" Michael couldn't bring himself to say the word.

Roxy inched forward slowly, her limbs weighed down by dread. She knew the answer to Michael's question before she even reached out to touch Dash, but she just couldn't make herself believe it. "No, no, no," she whispered under her breath. She touched Dash's arm with a brush of her fingertips. It was cold.

"How . . . how could this happen?" said Michael, but Roxy couldn't answer him. Her voice had deserted her. All she could do was stare at Dash. Was she still asleep, and this was some kind of nightmare? Blood rushed through her ears.

Moments later, everyone in the hotel arrived, drawn by the sound of Michael's cries. Ada shrieked. Lily turned ashen. Sylvia gasped. Nat pressed her palm across her mouth. Even Elijah, alerted by the noise that he could hear across in his bakery, arrived at the entrance to Dash's room and put his palm to his forehead in horror. Everyone was shocked to the bone.

Only Evangeline had the presence of mind to act. She stood, grimly silent until, with her voice quiet and level, she said, "I think we better call Johnson."

CHAPTER ELEVEN

DETECTIVE JOHNSON LOOKED ready to burst with rage. He was an intimidating presence at the best of times, but when he arrived at the Funky Cat just minutes after Evangeline had phoned him, his large body was so taut that it looked as though his muscles might snap at any moment.

They had closed the door to the room where Dash's body lay. No one could bear to look at him, and they congregated in the upstairs hallway in a silent huddle. Michael had stopped crying and was pacing back and forth, shaking his head. He was almost as white as Dash was. Evangeline and Roxy stood by the window, Roxy staring out of it blankly. Sylvia sat on the stairs with Nat, her arms around Nat's shoulders, while next to them was Elijah. He leaned his elbows on his knees and stared at the floor. Lily was slightly aloof and leaned against the wall a few feet from the others. Even Ada didn't have anything to say.

Johnson exploded up the stairs. "Another death? What is this? The Doomsday Hotel?" he raged. "This *cannot* be real."

Roxy was too stunned to speak, but Evangeline didn't have the same reserve. Her brow furrowing, she spat out, "How can you . . ."

But Johnson was not in the mood to be interrupted. "This is starting to look very suspicious, Ms. Evangeline, Ms. Reinhardt. Very suspicious indeed. This is the second dead body found in or around your hotel in the space of a few months. Is there something going on here that I should know about?"

A small wave of energy rippled through the group of influencers for whom reports of an earlier death was news. No one said anything, but a look here, a shift in posture there, indicated they had heard what Johnson had said and taken note. Roxy couldn't believe the audacity of the man. He was trash-talking her business in front of guests, *her* guests, the people essential to the business' success. Even for him, it was a new low.

In the past, in the face of such hostility and humiliation, she would have cowered and willed herself to disappear, but this was the *new Roxy*. Outraged, she drew herself up to her full height, which wasn't too tall in truth but was the best she could do. "Detective," she said sternly. "This is Michael, Dashiell Davies' best friend and business partner. It was Michael who found Dash's body. What do you have to say about that?"

Michael turned to the detective and stared him down with a look so penetrating it would have pierced right through anyone else. But Johnson was unfazed. "Humph. I'm sorry for your loss, but it's not my job to be your therapist," he said. "It's my job to investigate, and if there are suspicious circumstances, to find out who did this and bring them to justice." Michael looked away and closed his eyes. Unperturbed, Johnson continued, "The next step is to secure the crime scene and get forensic evidence. I will be interviewing y'all personally." He stared at Roxy and squinted. "Especially you. Don't you think it's a coincidence that all of these deaths started happening when you rocked up in town?"

"That's so unfair!" Nat burst out. Roxy was touched that Nat was sticking up for her. Nat's expired visa and her questionable immigration status meant that she usually tried to fade into the background whenever the police were around. "Of course this has nothing to do with Roxy!" Nat continued. "Why would it? She's just trying to live her life and run this hotel the best she can."

"A touching, if irrelevant, story," Johnson said.

But Nat wasn't to be dismissed. "This is a very serious situation and very stressful for our business. We would appreciate it if you didn't go around accusing us at every opportunity!"

"Look, do you think we can focus on what's *important* here? Like the fact that my friend and business partner is lying *dead* in his bed!" Michael cried. Chastened, Nat looked down at her feet. Not chastened at all, Johnson ignored him.

"So where's the body?" he asked. Roxy pointed to the bedroom door a few feet away. "Okay, everyone," he continued. "Go downstairs and get ready for questioning. I am going to bring the forensics team in now. None of you must be in this area." They all waited for what he would say next, and he glared back at them as if they were idiots. "Well, go on then. Get a move on!" Obediently, they all trooped downstairs. All, that is, except Roxy and Ada.

Ada faced Johnson squarely and put her perfectly manicured hand on her hip. "There's no way I am going down there without changing into something more appropriate."

She gestured down at her blue sundress. "This is not a suitable thing to wear after a death."

Johnson looked at her as though she were a one-eyed, many-limbed alien. "Excuse me?" he said in a tone that would shut down anyone else.

"My father has links with the Chief of Police and Prosecutions in Nigeria," Ada said. "I will not be told what to do by some provincial, small-town detective."

Roxy felt herself shrink a couple of inches. Johnson's eyes gleamed nastily.

"Ada," Roxy said in a half-warning, half-laughing tone. Was an influencer with a fan base of nearly three-quarters of a million about to be thrown in a New Orleans city police cell? An influencer who was only here because Roxy had invited her? She half-expected Johnson to charge Ada with obstructing a police investigation.

"I think you should stop right there, Miss," Johnson said, side-eyeing Ada and squinting as he assessed the creature before him.

But Ada did not stop. "I think you are a bad boy," she said, wagging her finger at him, "a very bad boy, throwing your weight around and accusing people. I know your kind. My father was targeted by your types when he became successful in business. His competitors wanted him out, but we Okafors do not bow to such pressure. There is nothing wrong with me going upstairs and changing my clothes. Or do you think that I might grab my Gucci handbag and kill someone on the way down? Or hide evidence in my Louis Vuitton carry-on? Types like you are absolutely ridiculous. Surely, if you let me go upstairs to change, that is not too much to ask? I will be back down within five minutes."

Johnson raised his chin. Ada's finger was still extended.

They were like two bulls in a standoff. For a moment, there was a tense silence. They glared at each other.

Johnson blinked first. "Do whatever you want," he growled. "I don't have time for this."

Ada's eyelashes quivered on hearing these words. She turned to float upstairs like a queen ascending a grand staircase, her head held high, dignified and victorious. Roxy's jaw almost dropped to the floor. It seemed the detective had met his match!

CHAPTER TWELVE

JOHNSON'S EXPRESSION WAS impassive, but as he tore his eyes away from Ada, he noticed that Roxy was still there. He gave a little jump, and his face turned an even deeper shade of purple. "What is it now?" he barked.

Roxy gulped but gathered herself to speak. She wanted to sound confident. She still didn't find confrontation easy, but she was getting braver at dealing with it. "I wanted to let you know we're in the middle of an Instagram campaign."

"A what?" he said.

"It's a marketing thing," Roxy explained.

"And what makes you think that interests me in the slightest?" he said. "Move. Go away. I need to enter this room, and I don't want you contaminating evidence."

"I need to let you know that," said Roxy, taking her cue from Ada and holding firm—just, "well, it's that my guests might photograph or video things. The people here are famous to their Instagram tribes. Between them, they have hundreds of thousands of followers. They make their living by producing videos and beautiful images. People watch them online. I wondered if it might interfere with the investigation." Roxy kept her voice even, but it was quivering a little.

Johnson looked incredulous. "Right," he said. "So the crazy modern world has finally infiltrated New Orleans, has it?" He sighed. "Today is a sad day, Ms. Reinhardt." He looked at Roxy disapprovingly as if she were personally responsible for this invasion. "I know nothing of this, and I don't *wish* to know anything of this. Just make sure to tell them that until I say so, there is to be no more photography or video. If they don't comply, they will be charged, and I will slap the handcuffs on them myself."

Roxy felt a shiver go through her. There was something about this man that got under her skin and made her want to run away as fast as possible in the other direction.

"Okay," she said. She managed to manufacture a smile. "I'll go and tell them now."

When she got downstairs, everyone except Michael was nibbling on beignets and sipping the brandy milk punch that Evangeline had made "for the shock."

"I can't believe that guy!" Nat said when she saw Roxy. "Who *does* he think he is? Why *does* he have to be so rude?"

"Will you pipe down, cher?" said Evangeline. "He's just doin' his job."

"No, I will not *pipe down*," Nat shot back. "Anyway, I don't see why you're defending him. He's not exactly your greatest fan, is he?" Evangeline sipped her punch and let out a deep long sigh.

"Johnson says that nobody is to record. No pictures, no video," said Roxy to the room.

Michael looked up from where he sat curled silently in an armchair. "How dare he," he said, quiet and deadly. "He can't tell us what we can and can't do in the wake of a tragedy. In any case, it's too late. I was recording an Insta-gram video when I went into Dash's room. The whole world knows about it already."

Roxy took a second to register Michael's comment before the full implications of what he was saying hit her. She put her hands to her head. "No, no, no," she whispered. If it weren't for the guests on every side of her, she would have crawled into a fetal position and rocked back and forth at this news. When she had considered the wisdom of the influencer campaign, the worst she imagined was a few bad reviews. She never considered the possibility that an unex-plained death would be beamed from her hotel live across the whole planet.

Just then, there was a series of knocks at the door that turned into a rain of hammer blows. Roxy practically jumped out of her skin. She flinched so hard that she elbowed Evangeline, who was standing next to her causing her to spill her punch on the floor.

"Oh sorry, sorry," Roxy said. "Who could that be?"

"It's probably the forensic team," said Lily. She looked coolly at Roxy. "Would you like me to answer?"

"No, no," said Roxy. "It's my responsibility." She felt like she was living a nightmare: an influencer dying in her hotel that was full of other influencers recording everything as a testimony. And she'd thought the Versace dress incident was bad enough.

Roxy walked into the hallway and with a sharp exhale opened the door. She expected to see people in white suits standing on the step with bags full of investigating equip-ment. Instead, the scene that greeted her when she swung open the heavy wooden door was far worse than that.

"Arghh!" She was blinded by a flash. Then another flash, then another. *Flash, flash, flash!*

"Roxy Reinhardt?" a woman shouted. A microphone was shoved into Roxy's face. A crowd of other men and women—all waving phones, cameras, notepads, pens, or microphones—pushed and jostled in front of her.

"Uh . . . yes?" she said, blinking. Roxy turned her head to protect her eyes from a flash only to be assailed by another. She was so stunned she couldn't move. She stood on the doorstep of the Funky Cat *Inn* protecting her eyes with her hand and noiselessly opening and closing her mouth like a goldfish as the frenzy in front of her refused to abate.

Suddenly, Roxy was grabbed from behind and pulled back into the hallway. Nat slammed the door shut and pressed her back against it for good measure. Only then did Elijah loosen his tight grip on Roxy's shoulders.

"Reporters!" Roxy cried. A couple of angry tears streamed down her face. She wiped them away furiously. "This is too much!"

Evangeline joined them. She shook her head. "No time for tears and shoutin', cher," she said. "We've got to make sure those reporters don't start puttin' cameras at the windows. You know they're goin' to be lookin' in from every angle.

"She's right, Roxy," Elijah said. "This is the hottest story out there right now, and I guarantee it's only going to get worse. My brother worked for a politician caught in a scandal and what those reporters will do for a story would make your short li'l blonde locks curl."

"But how can that be?" said Roxy. "We found him dead barely ten minutes ago."

"It was live on Instagram," said Nat. "This is a huge story."

"One that's only goin' to get bigger," said Evangeline. "A

virus, isn't that what you called it? The news will spread like wildfire. He was a celebrity of sorts, right? This isn't gonna go away, cher. You need to face it."

Roxy felt trapped. She could hear the clamor of reporters outside. "But what about when we want to go out?" she said. "What if they push their way in?"

"For now we're stuck inside unless the police decide to help us out on that score." Evangeline threw her eyes up to the ceiling. "And I doubt *that* very much." Roxy felt sick to her stomach.

Evangeline was not generally a hugging type of person, but now she put her arm around Roxy and patted her shoulder. "None of this is your fault, cher," she said kindly. "Don't be too hard on yourself, and don't get caught up in too many emotions, y'hear? You need to stay strong for the guests and make sure that everyone is okay. The world is watchin'. We can turn this around. Guests remember what you do when there is a problem much more than when everythin' goes well. Lemons to lemonade, cher."

"She's right, Roxy. Give the world an excellent impression of the hotel, despite being at the center of a crisis. You can do it. We've all worked too hard to give up now." Elijah snapped his fingers and sashayed in a tight circle around the lobby, his head rocking from side to side.

As she watched him, Roxy instantly felt better. Evangeline was right. Roxy had read in *The Hotelier,* the #1 industry magazine, that the level of service a hotel provided when a guest had a problem and was upset created the strongest impression. Well, the Funky Cat certainly had a problem now and her guests were certainly upset.

Summoning the strength from somewhere, Roxy clapped her hands together with a burst of energy. She was being looked to for leadership. "Let's show them that we can handle a crisis, the *worst* kind of crisis. Come on, people!" She didn't feel quite as confident as she sounded, but she was determined to take another crack at turning the situation around. She was going to take charge. She was going to *do this.*

CHAPTER THIRTEEN

WHILE DETECTIVE JOHNSON questioned the guests and staff, the forensics team were let in to the hotel and got to work. Johnson gave the press a stern warning not to come inside, and almost blocked Sage too, but eventually let her in. She, together with Nat and Elijah, worked to cover up the windows with trash bags secured with white strips of tape. This made Roxy feel sad.

"My gorgeous boutique hotel looks like it's in the middle of a war zone or in the path of a hurricane that's about to pass through," she said.

"Yeah, it looks and feels completely and utterly *wrong*, but it's necessary," Elijah said. When the chips were down, Elijah, for all his flouncing, custom cupcakes, and proclivity for partying could be pretty practical. "It won't be for long. We'll all be here to tear it down when this is over, and those horrible reporters have gone away."

Unable to leave, the guests and staff played board games and charades, and Evangeline kept everyone's spirits up with a never-ending supply of punch and café au lait. She rustled up po' boys and salad for lunch. Eventually, they all dispersed for an early afternoon nap, leaving Roxy alone in the lounge.

She sat down in a squishy armchair, her chin propped on her fist. There was a little squeak, and she looked down to see that Nefertiti had joined her. The fluffy white cat wound her body between Roxy's legs, the softness of her fur soothing her owner like a blanket. Roxy bent over to pick her cat up and plop her in her lap.

"Nef-nef, I'm trying to be brave. I'm trying to keep my spirits up. But it's hard, you know?" She stuck her nose into Nefertiti's fur and lay her cheek on the cat's back. It was like lying on the softest of soft white pillows.

"Come on, girl. Let's tidy this place up." Roxy stood and, with a mewl of protest, Nefertiti was dropped to the wooden floor.

As Roxy was picking up the used plates, Detective Johnson appeared. He looked grumpy and was chewing on a pen.

"Would you like something to eat, Detective?"

"Uh, no," Johnson said. As an afterthought, he added, "Thanks."

Roxy waited for him to say something, but when Johnson continued to chew on his pen, she asked, "Are you done here now? Can we get on with things?"

The detective sighed. "Yeah, seems no one saw or heard anything. According to them, they were all in their beds until morning. We'll see what they have to say down at the morgue about the cause of death, but you can go about your day. Just don't let anyone leave town until we know more about what happened here." Johnson appeared distracted. He made to leave, before turning back to face Roxy. "Tell me," he said wagging his pen at her. "There was a half-eaten cupcake on a plate beside the deceased's bed. And a thermos with the dregs of something milky inside it. There was a faint whiff of liquor. What was that?"

"We gave the influencers personalized cupcakes and brandy milk punch as a nightcap last night."

"And was that the last thing the deceased would have eaten?"

"I guess."

"Who was involved in preparing it?"

"Elijah made the cupcakes and N–Nat . . ." It suddenly dawned on Roxy where this line of questioning was going. She cleared her throat. "Nat made the punch and delivered it along with the cakes to the guests' rooms." Johnson eyebrows shot up, and he tapped his pen against his lips, a small smile forming.

"Surely you aren't suggesting that the nightcap had something to do with Dash's death?" Roxy asked in a here-we-go-again voice. "Or that Nat or Elijah were involved in some way?"

"Let's wait for the post mortem results before speculating, shall we, Ms. Reinhardt?" Johnson wagged his pen at her again, but his skeptical expression told Roxy that he clearly wasn't following his own advice.

By the time Johnson and his forensic team had left and Dash's body had been removed, it was evening. After checking that everyone was all right, Roxy decided to go for an evening jog. She thought it might clear her head. The press corps was still on her doorstep, but those who had hung around the back seemed to have given up. Roxy slipped out of the back door. When she set out, the sunlight was just beginning to fade, leaving a purply haze that felt a little eerie. As she ran, her feet rhythmically pounded the sidewalk while her mind wandered.

Roxy had grown up with a mother who put her down, who had never believed that Roxy was destined for any kind of happiness or success. In her head, Roxy could hear her mother's voice.

Why did you believe that you could have a good life, that things would get better, that you could be successful? Can't you see that everything you touch turns to dust?

Roxy knew that if her mom was with her right now, she'd get a knowing look followed by, "*Roxy, why did you even try to do that? You never finish anything you start. You should have played it safe.*"

But Roxy had not wanted to play it safe, not any longer. She had wanted to break with the past. She had tried her best to turn the Funky Cat Inn into a thriving business, tried to create, tried to succeed. And it had gone well for a while. But now look what had happened. Things were turning out worse than she could ever have imagined. Would she have been better to play it safe in the first place, like her mother would have said?

But it was too late to be second-guessing herself now. Evangeline had handed management and partial ownership of the Funky Cat over. Roxy had staff and suppliers who were relying on her. The Instagram campaign was underway. There was no way out but through. She needed to step up.

Back at the Funky Cat, after a shower, Roxy fell into a fitful sleep, waking several times in the night, horrible thoughts riding around her head and trampling all over her soul. Images of Ada wagging her finger and Johnson arguing swam in front of her eyes while the sound of Michael crying for help rang in her ears. It felt like someone had reached into her chest, grabbed her heart, and squeezed. But amid the chaos, she saw her friends—Sam, Nat, Elijah, Sage, and Evangeline—urging her on, telling her not to give up. Even Nefertiti made an appearance.

CHAPTER FOURTEEN

THE NEXT MORNING, there was no time to be dragged down by the trauma of the previous day. Roxy knew that it was her responsibility to make sure at the very least that the influencers were all right *and* that no further negative impressions of her hotel were going out into the world. She planned to make sure the reputation of the Funky Cat wouldn't be torn to shreds on her watch if she could possibly help it.

She got up, washed her face, and smiled at herself in the mirror. "I can do this," she said to herself. "I can, I can, I will, I must." She felt a little blip of depression catch her heart, a little reminder of the obstacles facing her, but she decided not to pay it any attention. She needed to be strong now, and strong she was going to be.

First things first, Roxy checked on Michael. He didn't come down for breakfast, and as Roxy went upstairs with a coffee and a plate of beignets, she had horrible visions of finding him in the same condition he had found Dash the previous day. Fortunately, that did not turn out to be the case. When she found him, Michael was sitting at the window in his room, staring out at the city. It was a gray morning, which obviously wasn't helping his mood.

"How are you doing?" asked Roxy, not knowing what else to say. She knew it was a dumb question, but it was hard to know what to say to someone whose best friend had just been murdered.

Michael said, "Oh fine, fine," in a dreamy, distracted voice. He seemed worlds away.

"Did you sleep all right?" she asked, setting the beignets and coffee next to him on the table.

"Terribly," he said. "All I could see was Dash's dead face looking back at me. I can't sleep here again."

Roxy nodded. "I understand. Why don't we get you to another hotel?" she said. "Maybe you'd be better staying at somewhere larger, more anonymous, and with more people around."

Michael looked at her for the first time since she entered the room. "That makes sense," he said flatly.

"If it weren't for Detective Johnson's orders you could go back home. You probably don't feel like being in New Orleans right now."

"Do you want me out of the way? Do you want me to leave so as not to inconvenience you anymore?"

"No, no!" Roxy said, horrified. "I was just thinking about your well-being.

Michael shook his head. His shoulders slumped. He leaned against the window. "You see? I just can't stay here. I keep wondering who would have done that to Dash and why." He got out his smartphone and showed it to Roxy. "That horrible detective released a statement to the news. Dash was poisoned. The police are treating his death as suspicious. Why would someone poison him? And how?

We all drank and ate the same things at dinner, didn't we? It just doesn't make any sense."

Roxy cringed inwardly on hearing this news and felt an ice-cold hand clutch at her heart. Was her food responsible? Was it the nightcap? Was there a murderer staying in her hotel? Would suspicion fall on her and her friends, *again*? She shook her head. "You're right. It doesn't make any sense."

Michael looked at her with a disbelief that he did not even care to veil. Roxy looked back at him, bewildered. "You don't think I . . .?"

"Sorry," he said. "No, I'm not sorry. I don't know if I'm sorry! It's just . . . anyone could have killed him. How am I supposed to know? How am I supposed to tell who's inno-cent and who's guilty?" He burst into tears. Great big sobs. "I'm so sorry, buddy!" he said through his wailing cries as he looked out of the window. "I'm so sorry!"

Roxy felt her heart might break listening to him. She rushed to kneel down in front of him and put her hands on his knees. It was an intimate gesture as if they were extremely good friends, but his cries reached deep into her heart and brought out all her compassion. "I am so, *so* sorry," she said. "But there was nothing you could have done. None of this is your fault."

"But it was!" he said. "It is! I was the one who convinced him that we should do this job here at your hotel. He didn't want to. This isn't his style. He wanted to go for the Hilton project. He wanted to focus on that. He was saying we should do a showreel to impress them. He even thought we should stay and shoot in Hilton Hotels on an unpaid basis to prove what we can do and get the job that way. But I told him no." Michael choked back a sob. "I told him, let's focus on our own indie stuff and not go running after a big name brand. And now look what's happened! It's all my fault, and nothing anyone can say will change my mind."

Roxy couldn't fathom what Michael was talking about, but she didn't feel it was the right moment to probe. She waited for him to continue speaking. She was willing to sit there and listen to him for as long as he wanted, but he shook his head and said, "I need to get out of here."

"I'll help you," Roxy said. "You want me to get you a reservation? Or parking? Or . . .? What do you need from me? I'm here for you." This was far beyond customer service. This was human to human. Roxy's heart was so heavy with compassion for Michael. She could not even begin to imagine what it must be like to have your best friend die, let alone find them dead, possibly murdered. She thought of what it might be like if she found Sam, Elijah, or any of her friends the way that Michael had found Dash, but her mind just wouldn't go there. She couldn't, wouldn't imagine it.

He said, "No, I'll take care of everything. All I need is for someone to get me over there so I don't throw myself in front of traffic."

That took Roxy aback. "I will go with you," she said quickly. "Tell me when you're ready."

"Now," he said, beginning to tap away at his phone. "I'm ready now."

CHAPTER FIFTEEN

"I'M JUST MAKING the booking," Michael said. "I'll go to the Hyatt. Then I'll see that awful detective and give him a piece of my mind. Why is he talking to the media before talking to me? I was Dash's business partner and his friend and . . ." He trailed off.

"I understand," said Roxy again. "Just remember that when we go out, there may well be reporters looking for you and perhaps me. We're two of the people who'll face the most press interest—me as the owner of the hotel and you as Dash's partner."

"Oh, man, I'd forgotten about that," said Michael. "I haven't thought of the outside world since the moment I found him. But I know my fans, Dash's fans, are out there, waiting. They need to hear from me, not a bunch of random reporters. It might seem crazy to go back on social media straight after this, but honestly, some of the fans are . . . well, they're like family. They need to hear from me." His face crumpled. "But I'm not strong enough yet." He sniffed and wiped his eyes.

"If they really care about you, they'll give you all the

time you need and will totally understand how you feel," said Roxy. "Just do it when you're ready."

Michael gave her a small smile. "Thank you so much for understanding, Roxy," he said. "I'm very hard on myself at times. It's wonderful to have a friend like you. Dash was . . ." His voice faltered.

Roxy felt her heart swell with warmth. "It's nothing," she said. "I'm glad to have met you. I just wish it had happened under better circumstances. Let's do what we can to get justice for Dash now. I promise I will fight to the end for him."

Roxy thought they should take a vehicle to the Hyatt. They could go in Sam's work van. They could hide in the back. But shortly after Sam said he was on his way, he called Roxy's phone. "The street's jammed with reporters and their cars," he said. "All over the place. They're parked in the middle of the street, everywhere."

"Have you tried the back entrance?"

"Yep, there's reporters there too."

"Let's just face them, Roxy," Michael said. "They want their pound of flesh, so let's give it to them. How bad can it be?"

Roxy thought it could be pretty terrible actually, but she said, "Okay, but no talking to them, promise?" Michael nodded.

So with Sam unable to make it through the throng, Michael and Roxy had no choice but to walk through a sea of reporters. They had to push their way through. There wasn't a single foot of space and none of the journalists would give an inch. Microphones were shoved in their faces. Questions were shouted in their ears. Someone even tried to wrestle Michael's case out of his hand. In response,

Michael elbowed the man in the chest to push him away. "Leave us alone!" Michael shouted.

Roxy winced. She pictured Michael looking like a crazy man on the front page of the newspaper. Perhaps they would even start to make up a narrative about Dash's killing, implicating Michael as the culprit. Trial by press, isn't that what they call it? Terrible. She didn't want to even think about what they'd print about her and her hotel.

Eventually, after much pushing and shoving and stonewalling, the pair arrived at the Hyatt. Thankfully, the reporters were barred from entering while Michael and Roxy were let through. The hotel locked the doors from inside once they'd passed into the lobby. Frustrated to have their quarry elude them without responding, the reporters piled up outside, banging on the glass. "We're going to call the cops on you!" a security guard shouted to the journalists, but it made absolutely no difference. The reporters were like a pack of wild wolves desperate to sink their teeth into their prey.

"Oof, this is what it must be like being part of a boy band. Thank you so much for coming with me," Michael said to Roxy breathlessly. They were both red-faced with exertion and adrenaline. "Those reporters were crazy. How are you going to get back?" Michael said.

Roxy looked out the door. "I think I'll have to get a police escort," she said with a sigh. Overhearing her, a young, bright, overly enthusiastic concierge said, "I can arrange that for you, miss."

"Thank you," Roxy replied hoping against hope that it wouldn't be Johnson who came to get her.

Michael's phone beeped, and he fished it from his pocket. His face clouded over as he read it. "I just got a message," he said. "It's Dash's family. Well, his mother and brother. His father died a long time ago. They're staying here until the case is solved. They're coming down from Missouri." His face was strained.

"Oh, I see," said Roxy. Then she ventured, "Is everything okay?"

"No, not really," Michael said. "They are not nice people, Roxy. They hate me and have wanted me out of Dash's life for a long time. They didn't trust him to live his own life, they wanted to dictate everything he did. But they didn't know him, they didn't *care* to know him, not the *real* him. They didn't understand what he wanted or what he loved. They just wanted to control him and have him conform, be a good, hometown boy who's great to his momma. He was never going to be like that, he wanted more from life, but they kept on trying."

Roxy gave a sad little smile. "He was about the furthest thing from a conformist you could imagine, wasn't he?"

"Tell them that when you see them," Michael said bitterly. "They thought he was being led astray by me." He gave a sad smile too. "It was probably the other way round, wasn't it?"

Roxy returned Michael's smile. "I think so, yes."

"Anyway, they're planning to stay at your hotel." He widened his eyes meaningfully. "Good luck."

CHAPTER SIXTEEN

UNFORTUNATELY FOR ROXY, it *was* Detective Johnson who drove her from the Hyatt back to the Funky Cat. He took the opportunity to drive her in a marked squad car complete with flashing lights and the occasional blast of the siren in order, she suspected, to make a spectacle of her and give her a stern warning.

"I heard that you've been saying that Dash was poisoned," she said to him.

"Yeah, that's right. At *your* hotel." Johnson kept his hands on the steering wheel but leaned over meaningfully, taking his eyes off the road and the reporters for a second to glance in her direction.

"Does that mean we can expect to be graced with your presence some more? Will you be coming to question us again?"

"And poke around your kitchen. We're waiting on the full toxicology reports, but your place was the last one where the victim ate or drank anything."

"Only along with everyone else!" Roxy said, her indignation overcoming her shyness. "And the rest of us are fine."

"Means nothing, we have to investigate thoroughly. The victim's food may have been messed with. And I want to talk to that flibbertigibbet again. The one from across the road."

"Elijah."

"Yeah, him. And that goth. The one with the tatts."

"You mean Nat."

"Yeah, her. I want to talk about them nightcaps. You likely have a murderer in the house."

Roxy frowned. She didn't like the sound of this at all.

Johnson was prattling on in the seat next to her. "Now, don't you go around investigating like you did last time, y'hear? I'll slap cuffs on you faster than you can say Miss Marple, if you do," he threatened. "We need to treat this very carefully, what with the press interest and all."

They lapsed into silence and neither of them said much else for the rest of the ride. Roxy stared out at the reporters clamoring at the patrol car's windows, fighting the misery that was weighing her heart down as they crawled along the street. What had her life become? Riding in police cars, chased by hordes?

It was only when she got back to the hotel and into the kitchen where Nat and Evangeline were clearing away breakfast that she realized her insides were turning over with hunger. She hopped onto a stool and ate beignet after beignet while watching Nat load the dishwasher.

"Johnson wants to talk to you again. He says Dash was murdered and that it was probably one of us. You were the last person to serve Dash food." Nat looked at her quizzically. "The nightcaps," Roxy explained.

"Oh right, well I'm totally in the clear. Unless someone's put rat poison in the punch when I wasn't looking, they were regular old brandy milk punches."

"Yeah, I know you didn't do anything," Roxy said mournfully. "But someone did. And probably someone who was here that night." Hopelessness was starting to wash over her like a tide on a beach. She kept pushing the emotion away but it kept returning. Each time it got a little bit stronger and pervaded a little bit further into her soul.

Nat regarded Roxy with a worried expression. "Look, I'm really sorry if anything I've done has made things difficult for you." She winced, then paused from loading the dishwasher, and turned to lean against the side. She gave a deep sigh. "I know I should have been nicer to Ada. About Ada . . . it's just that . . . well, everything is changing. I've never been a person who is good with change. Do you know what I mean?"

"Oh, I've forgotten all about the dress incident. That seems like an age ago now and, well, we're both in the same boat," said Roxy. "I don't like change either."

"What do you mean?" Nat said. "You seem to revel in it. You're sure fancy enough around this place, always wearing your lovely sparkly outfits, smiling like it's Mardi Gras."

"You're plenty good enough as you are," said Roxy, smiling. "Isn't that right, Evangeline?"

"I don't know what you're both talkin' about," the older woman said. "You young ones and all your soul-searchin' are a mystery to me. Back in my day we were hired for a job and we did it, no questions asked, no navel-gazin' required."

"That's all very well for you to say, Evangeline," said Nat. "You don't live in the age of social media. Everything is about identity now. Everyone has to have their own personal brand. It's not easy. It brings with it a whole bunch of insecurities and worries that we are not matching up to everyone else." She popped her head out into the dining room to check that there were no guests there. She lowered her voice to a shouted whisper. "Like Lily Vashchenko. She's just so perfect! Her home is immaculate and beautiful. She always has the best outfits on, and her hair is amazing. And that's before we even consider her social media content! How are we supposed to match up to *that*? That series she did on other people's kitchens was tremendous."

Evangeline shook her head. "Why would you want to look at pictures of other people's kitchens for goodness sake? How do people even have the time?"

Nat sighed. "You just don't get it."

"You're right about that, cher," Evangeline said. "I don't. And I have no wish to."

Roxy continued to munch away at beignet after beignet, amused at the conversation but feeling heavy-hearted still. "He wants to poke around the kitchen some more too," she said.

"Who does?" Evangeline asked.

"Johnson."

"Hmph! It wasn't my food that poisoned that Dash fella!" Evangeline grumbled.

"No, I'm sure it wasn't. We'd all be dead if that were the case, but maybe whatever poisoned him was put *in* the food. He's right, it's not outside the realms of possibility that someone tampered with it." Roxy put her half-eaten beignet down, her stomach finally signaling that it had had enough. She pushed herself from her stool. "I want us to do something," she said. "Moping around is not helping. One of us may be the murderer, but the rest of us are innocent. I have to keep things positive. I can't give up."

"There's the evening with Sage coming up. She's bringing her crystals and cards and whatnot," Nat said.

"I know, but that's not until tomorrow. I want to do something *now*. I have to shift this energy that's weighing me down."

"Once I'm finished up here, I was looking at hitting a couple of flea markets," said Nat. "I want to find some more furniture to upcycle."

"But everything's done!" said Roxy. "The hotel décor is complete."

Nat got a mischievous glint in her eye. "It'll never be done. Not if I've got anything to do with it," she said. "I have a great idea for a piece in the dining room that's going to take the luxury quotient to a whole new level."

Roxy smiled. When Nat put her heart and soul into things, it was always a fun time. "Come on, share with the class, then."

"Nope," Nat said with a cheeky grin. "You'll have to wait and see."

"Why don't we ask Lily Vashchenko to come along with us? She's turned upcycling around. It used to be something you'd do when you were broke. Now it's a virtue signal," Roxy said. "Isn't she the upcycling Queen?"

Nat pouted. "No! I am!"

"Okay, okay," Roxy said, her palms up. "You *do* know what you're doing, I'll give you that. But you don't have nearly a million Instagram followers just yet, do you?"

"Nope, and I never will," said Nat. "The idea of being famous makes my skin crawl, *especially* considering what's going on right now."

"Very sensible, cher," said Evangeline. "More trouble than it's worth. You run along now, I'll finish up here."

"Thanks, Evangeline!" said Nat. She ran out of the room at a sprint, anxious to be on her way.

Lily Vashchenko was delighted by the invitation to visit

the flea market. At least she smiled, enigmatic and cat-like as usual. "I wonder if I'll find any unique New Orleans pieces," she said. "The architecture around here is very interesting. Perhaps I'll find something wonderful to put in my own home."

Roxy called up to Sylvia's room to see if she wanted to join them, but there was no reply.

"I think I saw her going out the back with those pole thingies of hers," Nat said. "What does she need them for anyway? It's not like she's going to be climbing any mountains."

"They'd be good defense in the event she comes upon any rabid reporters though," Roxy responded. Nat nodded in agreement.

The three of them assembled in the lobby and Roxy peered through the front door spyhole. Most of the reporters had given up and dispersed. "They probably followed Johnson to the station after he escorted me back here in a squad car. He's the only one talking to the press about what happened. Come on, there's hardly anyone outside. Let's go before we change our minds!"

CHAPTER SEVENTEEN

ROXY, NAT, AND Lily set out together on foot. There were still dribs and drabs of reporters on the sidewalk. "Walk straight past them, don't answer any questions. Don't even look at them. Just pretend like they're not there," Roxy told Nat and Lily.

They only planned to walk as far as Sam's laundry. They took a couple of back streets and managed to lose most of the reporters that trailed them. By the time they reached their destination, there was only one still following them, and he was content to stand at the street corner and watch.

"Sam!" said Roxy, with relief, as they burst into the laundry, the constant whirring of the machines making a loud hum. It was hard to make herself heard. Sam was loading a machine, but he stopped when he saw the trio come in.

"Hey! How are you?"

"Um, well, it's been quite a day so far," she said. "I took Michael to the Hyatt, and the press chased us, and I had to have a police escort home and now . . ."

"Are you okay?" His eyes were soft with concern, and

he came toward her as if to hug her, but then thought better of it and backed away.

Roxy felt heat rise to her cheeks. "Oh fine, fine," she said. "Don't worry about me. I'm just concerned about Michael and the rest of the guests, and now Nat and Elijah because Johnson is taking a hard look at them because of the nightcaps, and oh well, we just wanted to get out and lose ourselves in a crowd. We want to go to the flea market. Do you think you could take us in your van?" She was babbling and she knew it.

"Oh," Sam said, wincing. "I'd be happy to, but I've just sent one of my guys out in it to collect an order. I guess . . ." He looked a little embarrassed. "We can go in the Rolls?"

"That would be fabulous," said Lily immediately.

"Fine with me," said Nat.

Roxy thought they might be a little conspicuous, but she grinned at him nonetheless. "You can take us by horse and buggy if you like. Just so long as we get there."

Sam grinned back, and the atmosphere between them lit up, so much so that Nat had to wave her arms between the two of them to break it up.

They went out the back entrance to the parking lot. Lily's slanted almond eyes widened when she saw Sam's maroon Rolls Royce. "Wow," she said, a rare enthusiasm animating her voice. "Now that's a real car. The laundry business must pay better than I thought."

Sam avoided eye contact with her and shoved his hands in his pockets. "Um . . . well . . ."

But Lily wasn't paying enough attention to realize how shifty he was being. She had her iPhone out and was snapping selfies of herself against the car at every angle. "This will look good to my fans," she said. "A Rolls Royce. That's style."

When they got inside, Lily admired the cream leather seats and ran her hands over the surface of them. "Goodness," she said. "If I capture the Hilton deal, maybe I will be able to cruise in one of these myself."

Something clicked in Roxy's brain. *First Michael, now Lily.* "The Hilton deal? What is that?"

"Oh, it's a huge contract," Lily said. "They're looking for an influencer to partner with for an enormous advertising campaign. It should last the whole of next year. I'm putting together a portfolio to impress them, and this visit with you is part of that. They're going for the young, upcoming luxury market. That's my target, and what you do fits in pretty well, which was why I was so keen to visit you," she said with a smile.

Roxy's palms began to sweat. *The Hilton deal.* The same deal that Dash and Michael had been going for! Lily, Michael, and Dash had been competitors. As they drove, Roxy looked at Lily out of the corner of her eye, studying her intently. Was she capable of murder? She seemed nice enough. She wasn't effusive or gregarious, rather cool, even unapproachable at times, but Roxy knew that appearances were not necessarily all that they seemed. Perhaps Lily had had something to do with Dash's death. Perhaps Dash and Michael were nearer to closing the deal than she was and she knew this. Perhaps Lily had picked Dash off. Perhaps, Roxy thought, she should find out.

Then she remembered Johnson's warning. He had seemed deadly serious. She was *not* to investigate. He had ordered her. Roxy reflected on what Lily had told her as she leaned back in her seat. Her theory made sense, but it seemed barely credible to conclude that this elegant, successful woman would murder someone for money. Roxy couldn't believe it and eventually, exhausted by events of the day and lulled by the sublime, if incongruous, ride to the flea market in Sam's Rolls Royce, she put the thought out of her mind and fell asleep.

After the flea market, Sam dropped Roxy, Nat, and Lily off back at the Funky Cat. The trio clambered out of the Rolls with their flea market finds. Nat had found a small, broken old table and a sculpture of a woman with a bow and arrow that was so chipped, Roxy couldn't conceive how on earth Nat was going to turn it into something that was even half-decent. All the reporters had gone now and Sage met the three women at the front door.

"Greetings to all," she said, her voice trembling. "Dash's family members are here. They are in the dining room."

It took a lot to rattle Sage. She'd done years and years of spirit and mindset training to make sure that she stayed tranquil and "aligned with the spirits," even in the most difficult of circumstances. Now though there was a look of fear in her eyes, and she was breathing a little more deeply than usual, as if she were trying to calm herself.

Roxy wondered what on earth could have upset Sage so, but her attention was dragged away by the need to face Dash's family. Roxy took a deep breath and plastered what she hoped was an appropriate expression on her face, sympathetic and kind, but *in charge*. She walked into the dining room with her head high and her stride firm.

There, sitting on one of the most luxurious couches in the lounge was a plump, attractive-looking, middle-aged woman, and a sickly, pale young man of about twenty-five.

The woman stood up with a smile that seemed rather broad under the circumstances, her hand outstretched for a handshake. "Hello, you must be Roxy Reinhardt," she said with all the formality of a businessperson closing a multi-million real estate deal. Roxy was taken aback. The woman didn't come across as a mother whose son had just been poisoned. Her hair was blown out, her long nails were bright red, and her lipstick matched her fingers. She wore high heels. There was a designer logo on her purse.

As Roxy scrutinized the woman carefully and slowly, a barely discernible sadness in her eyes became apparent. Her polished exterior, to Roxy at least, was a façade, one that was brittle and which Roxy suspected could break down at any moment.

"My name is Kathy, and I'm Dash's mother." Her smile fell for a moment before she pulled it back into place. "This is my younger son, Derek."

The young man next to her did not stand up and had none of his mother's charm. He was wearing a hoodie pulled too far forward; it partially obscured his face. When his mother spoke, he stayed seated in his chair and peered out from under too-long bangs, fiddling with a model airplane in his lap.

"My little Derek is pretty shy," the woman said, proudly. She looked at her son affectionately as if he were ten years old. "We are going to stay here until Dash's . . . killer . . . has been caught. You won't get rid of us for quite a while probably." She started laughing, but in a moment, her laughter turned to sobs. Composing herself quickly, she gave a huge snort and wiped her eyes. "Sorry, you'll have to excuse me," she said. "It's a difficult time."

"Of course it is," said Roxy kindly. "Please, *please* do stay for as long as you'd like, and ask me if you need anything. Has Sage shown you up to your rooms yet?"

"Yes, she has. Thank you," said Kathy.

"I'm staying in Dash's room," said Derek, suddenly coming to life. "To be close to him."

"He knew where it was and everything," said Sage. She had a strange look on her face. "Something must have called out to you, Derek," she said.

"Now I just have one thing to tell you," said Kathy. She maneuvered herself close to Roxy and lowered her voice. "You've got to understand that that horrible Michael was a terrible influence on Dash. He got my son involved in all sorts of shady things. I'll tell you the story of how they met . . . Well, maybe not now, maybe another time, someplace private, but let's just say that Michael, well, he's not *good news*. I'm glad he's not here. I couldn't stay here if he were. I wouldn't be surprised if he were involved somehow in my son's death. After all, they split the business fifty-fifty. Michael stood to gain a lot if Dash weren't around.

"I . . . I . . . I . . . Well, perhaps you should be telling this to the police, not me," Roxy said, waving her hands in front of her. "I'm not an investigator. I hear what you're saying, and I'm so sorry for your loss, but if you want to speak about the case, I think you'd better talk to Detective Johnson."

"I will," said Kathy. "Soon. I'm just warning you, don't get involved with Michael, and don't listen to any of his stories. He's not a good man. Trust me." Her blue eyes pierced Roxy. "Just trust me on that."

CHAPTER EIGHTEEN

"DASHIELL WAS MY darling boy," Kathy Davies said the next morning. It was Sunday, and she was standing in front of the congregation in a packed church, St. Joseph's. Kathy, showing phenomenal organizational skills, had organized a memorial service for her son in just a few hours and the viral communication properties of Instagram had done the rest. Every seat was taken, and all the aisles were chock full of people in bright T-shirts, just like the ones Dash used to wear. The shirts had been Michael's idea. The press had been banned, but reporters congregated around the door outside, like bees around a honeypot.

"He was a good soul and a good boy," Kathy continued. "He had a bright future ahead of him. He was going to quit playing around on YouTube and Instagram, jaunting all over the world. He was planning to settle in his hometown, and live close to his momma." The crowd murmured at this news but quickly settled down.

"It's lies," Michael whispered furiously to Roxy as they sat next to each other in one of the hard pews. "All lies. He couldn't stand her. All she wanted was to control him, just like she controls Derek."

Roxy listened to Michael's words, but she was still a little wary of him after what Kathy had said. She truly didn't know who to believe.

"But he wasn't quick enough to make that decision and look what happened," said Kathy. "I don't want any of you to make the same mistake. If you have a family who loves and adores you, go *home* to them. Don't go running around the world chasing butterflies, and putting yourself in danger. You might just end up . . ." her eyes welled with tears, "in a casket."

Another murmur rippled through the crowd. Michael got up and stormed toward the entrance. Roxy followed him. She had to push and shove through the sea of bright colors to make it through. When she got outside, it was like she'd been underwater and had finally surfaced, gasping for breath. Around her, fans who had been unable to fit in the church milled around. Roxy and Michael hid among them, catching their breath until a group of reporters spied them and came rushing forward. It was an ambush and not a little scary.

"Get away from me!" Michael hollered.

Roxy looked around, trying to find a spot where they'd be left alone, but there wasn't one. There was only a large cemetery to the right, where reporters hung around on the paths between the gravestones, and a wide row of stores to the left. The street in front of the church was blocked with vehicles.

"Come on," Roxy said. She grabbed Michael's hand, and they took off running through the vehicles and into the streets beyond.

Soon they let go of each other's hands and flew through

the backstreets of New Orleans independently. They heard the pounding of footsteps as journalists ran behind them, trying to catch up, but the pair kept running and running until Roxy felt a pain in her side.

Finally, they reached the Funky Cat. The courtyard was deserted. The front door to the hotel was locked, even though Roxy knew Nat was in there with Evangeline and Sage and Elijah. They were preparing for the influx of fans they were expecting after the service.

Roxy hammered on the door, hoping there were no reporters close behind. No one answered. She scrambled to get her phone out of her pocket and called Nat. "Let us in!" It would take too long to go around the back.

Within moments the door was open. Michael and Roxy darted inside.

"That woman!" Michael said as soon as he had gotten his breath back. "She's crazy! Seriously, Dash and her didn't get on. He respected her because she was his mother, he went to visit and was kind to her, but man, if she'd had her way, he'd be living his life in a prison of her making. Did you see Derek? He's like a shell, like a ghost of a person. She dictates his whole life. She won't even let him have a girl-friend. Dash said Derek had one once, and his mom sabo-taged it so bad the girl left town and never came back."

Roxy shook her head not knowing what to say. Family troubles weren't her forte. They made her uncomfortable.

"And did you *hear* what she said about dreams, oh excuse me, *chasing butterflies*? Don't do that, or you'll end up dead? That was the total *opposite* of how we lived life. Dash and me, we lived *only* for chasing our dreams."

Michael fell down onto one of the chairs in the lobby, his legs splayed, his hands dangling over the arms of the chair. "Maybe she's right, though. If we hadn't been following our bliss, none of this would have happened. If we'd stayed home like good little boys, gotten regular jobs, and stopped reaching for the stars, Dash might still be alive. Maybe following your dreams *is* dangerous."

"I don't think so . . ." said Roxy. His declaration had her thinking. If *she* hadn't gone for her dreams, leaving her life behind to come to New Orleans and taking up management of the hotel, she certainly wouldn't now be mixed up in a murder investigation. But then again, she wouldn't be having the adventure of her life either, wouldn't be making great new friends, wouldn't be learning, living, and loving it. She'd be stuck in a dead-end job with a succession of dead-beat boyfriends, most likely.

Michael shook his head. "No. Dash never believed in living smaller than you dreamed. He'd have preached, 'Go out there and get it, whatever it is!'" He thumped the arm of his chair. "I should keep his legacy alive." But then he shook his head. "No. No, I shouldn't. He's dead now. Who'd take life advice from a dead guy?"

"Let me ask you a question," said Sage.

Roxy jumped and turned around—she hadn't realized Sage was there. She was standing in the doorway in flowing blue robes and a serene expression.

"Sure," Michael said, his face a picture of torment.

"If you could speak to him now—to Dash," a mystical look crossed Sage's face, "do you think he would regret the way he lived? Do you think he would wish that he had bent to his mother's wishes?"

Michael thought for a moment. "No, I don't think so, not at all."

"Do you think he'd still believe in chasing one's dreams, spiritual expansion, achievement, and fulfillment?"

"Yes," Michael said, his eyes brightening a little, and his face settling, more relaxed. "Yes, I do."

Sage said nothing more. She turned and went back into the dining room without a word.

After a few moments of silence, Nat came over to Roxy and said quietly, "I think you're going to have to help us. We're really behind."

"Okay," said Roxy. "Michael, I need help with preparing the food for our guests. They'll be here for the wake soon. Are you okay with me doing that? Do you want me to stay with you? Is there anything you need?"

"I'll come and help," he said.

"Oh, you don't have to," said Roxy.

"I *want* to," Michael insisted, and Roxy could see that it would help, so she let him.

CHAPTER NINETEEN

THEY SET ABOUT finishing up preparations for the wake. A buffet comprising some of the best food New Orleans had to offer—gumbos and jambalayas, rice and vegetables seasoned and spiced to Creole perfection—was laid out. Tiered cake stands were stacked high with Elijah's pastries, and coffee stations stood at the ends of the tables along with condiments, cream, liqueurs, and spirits. To create the right atmosphere, Nat would sing some light, soulful jazz and a few of Dash's favorite tunes accompanied by Sam on his saxophone.

"It looks fabulous," Elijah said.

Roxy looked around. "It does, doesn't it? We're doing Dash proud." She looked at Elijah and leaned in. "Look, Elijah, are you worried about Johnson investigating you? He means to look carefully at your cupcakes."

Elijah laughed. "I'd like to see him try!"

"But seriously, Eli, Dash ate your cupcake. It was the *last* thing he ate."

Elijah shrugged. "I've been making pastries since I was knee-high to a grasshopper. I've not poisoned anyone yet.

And besides, everyone got one. They'd all be dead if I messed up."

"That's what Nat said."

Elijah clasped Roxy firmly by the shoulders and looked into her eyes. "It'll be fine. You don't seriously think Nat or me interfered with his nightcap do you?"

"No, but . . ."

"Well, then. The police will catch the real killer and everything will go back to the way it was. You'll see."

Roxy wished she had as much confidence as Elijah clearly had.

"Look, I've got to go back across to the bakery. You can send the overflow there if you become overrun." He drew his wiry body up to his full height and clapped his hands like a male flamenco dancer. "It's time to *partay!*"

"Elijah, please. It's a wake," Roxy said.

"Trust me, Rox, it'll be a party." Elijah turned with a flourish and returned to his bakery to await the crowd.

Elijah was right. Before Roxy knew it, everyone from the church had descended on the Funky Cat, and she and the others were rushed off their feet serving guests and replenishing the buffet. They were deluged with so many people that many of them overflowed onto the cobbled street outside while others crammed into Elijah's bakery. Weaving and bobbing through them all, Elijah carried trays of pastries high above his head, serving them to anyone who wanted one.

The light, soulful jazz Nat had planned to sing gave way to a blistering rendition of *Chattanooga Choo Choo* when a guest showed up with a trumpet. The crowd contributed improvised train sound effects and even a beatboxer joined in! Dancing and toasts and stories and jokes, all in memory of Dash Davies, continued into the late afternoon. "I told you," Elijah said to Roxy afterward.

Three hours later, as the event started to wind down, Roxy noticed an empty spot on one of the couches. She took the opportunity to flop down into it, exhausted. She'd been running around with food and drinks, meeting her guests' wide range of needs for the entire time. She had had to eject some people out of a bedroom at one point. They were admiring it, but still.

As she plopped down, she happened to sit between Sylvia Walters and Ada Okafor, who didn't seem to be making much of an effort to talk with each other.

"Hi, Roxy," said Sylvia. "You look exhausted." She was wearing a navy T-shirt and khaki cargo pants. A bright orange neckerchief was tied around her head. She pointed to it. "Out of respect for Dash."

"That's nice. Yes, exhausted," said Roxy. "But it's all worth it to honor Dash."

Ada was sitting on the couch like a movie star. She was wearing a long, vivid, pink gown that trailed to the floor. There was a glass of champagne in her hand, and again her nails were perfectly manicured to match her outfit.

"It is very sad," she said to Roxy. She even sounded like she meant it a little.

"Yes," Roxy said. She looked around the room. "He seems to have led a very full life, though. His message certainly spread far and wide."

"Indeed. I was not a fan of his silly nature, but never mind." Ada's face was expressionless, and she sipped her champagne in a serious manner.

Roxy looked at her out of the corner of her eye. She knew that Ada had felt humiliated by the dress incident even though Roxy was sure that Dash had spilled his wine by accident. Nevertheless, it had happened in front of her fans, all of *his* fans, and perhaps any of Nigerian high society who happened to be watching. Had Ada been unhinged enough by that to kill him?

Roxy wanted to ask a probing question but wasn't sure whether to. She thought for a moment. "You two weren't the best of friends, were you?"

"He spilled red wine all over my white Versace. You wouldn't be happy, either. It was a limited edition, you know."

"Yes, so you said." There was a pause during which Roxy held Ada's gaze as she wondered about the possibility of Ada being a murderer.

Ada suddenly jumped. She put her hand to her chest. "You're not implying that *I* had anything to do with his death, are you?"

"No, no, of course not!"

"I am a very religious woman, Roxy," Ada said. "Just because a person believes in Louis Vuitton it does not mean she cannot believe in God also. I am very forgiving and would never harm anyone, much less for a prank. I am medically trained, remember."

"Sorry," said Roxy. "I didn't mean anything by it."

"I should hope not."

The atmosphere felt so uncomfortable that Roxy had to leave. "Well, you'll have to excuse me, I have to go check on the next crawfish boil," she said.

She didn't know why, intuition perhaps, but as soon as Roxy reached the small room at the back of the kitchen, she checked Ada's Instagram profile. She whipped out her phone and loaded the page. There was a gorgeous picture of Ada posing at her dressing table in her room at the Funky Cat. Roxy wondered how she had done it—it was so good, it looked like a professional shot. The caption simply said, 'Condolences.' Ada wore a grave expression, but she looked like a model posing for a designer brand rather than someone about to attend a funeral service. It seemed to Roxy to be extraordinarily inappropriate. That there was no picture or mention of Dash, merely compounded her confusion.

Roxy scrolled through the comments. Some said:

```
RIP Dash.
```

But many more were commenting on how beautiful Ada looked and the exquisiteness of the dress she was wearing. One even said:

```
Condolences. Ha ha ha! He deserved what he
     got after what he did to you.
```

Roxy noticed something else too. Ada had tapped the red heart next to each and every comment. She had "loved" them all, even the nasty ones.

CHAPTER TWENTY

"**P**HEW, IT'S A busy day," Roxy told Nat.

"You're telling me," Nat replied. They had cleared the debris from the morning's wake and were now preparing for the evening entertainment.

Roxy had planned what she was calling an "Evening of Love and Light" for the influencers. Whenever anyone came to New Orleans, they always wanted to know about the spiritual influences and who better to introduce them to New Orleans's mystical realm than Sage?

"Sage has persuaded Dr. Jack at the botanica to bring along a selection of magical supplies and a pile of crystals of all types," Roxy told Nat. The Englishwoman looked up at her boss, her lips pressed into a thin line. Nat was on her hands and knees in the dining room sweeping under a corner unit with a hand brush. Nat didn't say anything, her silence speaking for her.

"What?" Roxy cried. "I loved crystals as a little girl. I desperately wanted a 'Grow Your Own Crystals' kit for my birthday one year. Of course, I didn't get it." Roxy was laying the table for the evening's dinner. "Did you know that if you drink the water that crystals have been in, you absorb their powers?" Nat rolled her eyes. "At least that's what Sage said," Roxy finished.

"I think she was having you on."

Before the evening began, however, Roxy, Sage, Elijah, and Sam headed over to the Hyatt to check on Michael. He'd spent most of the afternoon following the memorial service sitting in a corner of the kitchen at the Funky Cat, avoiding his fans, his mood successfully repelling them for the most part. He'd gone back to the Hyatt for a nap.

"I'll take him his very own goodie bag of botanical items," said Sage. "The poor soul is in a bad place. He needs the spirits now more than ever." She found a basket in the kitchen and made up a hamper of sorts with candles, an oracle deck, sparkling pastel crystals, colored stones, a notebook with 'Magic' written on the front, some beaded necklaces, and incense.

When they arrived at his room, Michael opened the door with groggy eyes. His face was so swollen with misery, he looked like he'd been in a boxing match. When he saw them, he pulled a robe around his body defensively, the untied belt trailing on the floor.

"Hello," he said flatly.

"Hi there," said Roxy. "If you need some time to yourself, we can leave. We just wanted to check on you."

Sage smiled. "And we brought you a gift, honey."

Sam smiled too. "I have nothing to give you, but a friend in need is a friend indeed and all that. I'm here for you, buddy."

"And I'm here should you wish to rock 'n' roll," Elijah said, pulling a dance move. "Otherwise, I'll shut up."

Michael looked at them all and gave them a small smile. "Come in."

Roxy expected the room to be a mess with clothes strewn everywhere and half-eaten room service food cluttering the table-tops. If she were to face the loss of a good friend, Roxy suspected that she would descend into chaos, but the room was the opposite of what she expected—it was as neat as a pin. Even the coffee cups and sachets on the side table were in perfect alignment as if Michael had spent time arranging them to be just so.

"Sit, please," Michael said, gesturing at the chairs by the window. He sat down on the bed. Elijah and Sage remained standing. Elijah was too full of energy to sit down while Sage stood tall with all the poise and elegance of a statue, her light gray robes flowing around her. Sam and Roxy sat on the chairs Michael had pointed to. Sage handed Michael the basket she had brought with her. "Michael, honey, this is the least we can do for you. Remember, it is in moments of deep pain that we are the most connected to the spiritual world. Shamans, they're spiritual doctors, will eat burning hot chili peppers without water. They incur great pain as they do, but they believe that in this way they can most securely contact the dead and any other spirit they want to connect with." It was not an approach Roxy would have taken, but Michael was enthralled.

Sage continued. "Alchemy is the ability to turn tragedy into victory. This is a tragedy for *us,* but know that Dash is on the other side, laughing and playing jokes, as usual. His spirit isn't gone. How could it be? I feel it now. Can't you, if you think of him? He's still around. He won't stay long, though. He's got to reincarnate and will soon choose where and when. He might go back to Source for a while to recharge, but then he will return in another form. But none of that technical detail matters. All I'm showing you is that his energy will go on and on. He lives forever. Like us all."

Roxy watched Michael's response to this carefully. She was skeptical of the idea about life after death, and she was ready to jump in if he responded poorly, but she also knew that to people who were grieving, sometimes these ideas helped.

"Thank you, Sage," Michael mumbled tearfully, looking at his hands. "I'd like to come tonight."

Sage's display of crystals was something to behold. It had a shining, other-worldly aura. Sage had taken one of the trestle tables that were usually put into service in the kitchen, covered it with a soft purple velvet cloth, and laid crystals all over it. They caught the light of the lamps around the lounge and twinkled and sparkled in the early evening light.

Roxy hovered by the table, staring at the crystals for ages. One, in particular, caught her eye. There was a heart-shaped pink stone in the middle of it. Other pink and clear stones radiated from the center in beautiful swirls.

"That one's for finding a happy romantic relationship," said Sage, coming up behind her. "Is that something you'd like?"

Roxy was quite taken aback. "Um . . . well, yes . . . But no! I mean, I love the stones, but I don't want a romantic relationship right now." She became acutely aware of where Sam was at that moment. He had just arrived and was on the other side of the room rigging up some fairy lights.

"Oh, right," Sage said, a little smile tugging at the corner of her lips. She flicked a glance in Sam's direction. "I under-stand. Well, when you're ready, I'll help you make a crystal grid. It'll help you generate one. A romantic relationship, I mean."

"That won't be any time soon, I can assure you!" Roxy said. "I'm much too busy." She laughed a little too loud. "But what about doing a crystal grid to ensure justice for Dash?"

"Aha! You read my mind, honey," Sage said. "When Michael arrives, I am planning to share it with him. Because he was close to Dash, if he's the one to put the crystals in place, it will have a stronger effect. Also, if . . ." She trailed off.

"If what?"

Sage drew closer and lowered her voice. "If he's *not* who he seems to be, he'll resist making the grid. He'll be *terrified*, and it'll show. Trust me."

CHAPTER TWENTY-ONE

ROXY FROWNED. "DO you think he might have . . .?"

"I don't know," said Sage. "My intuition is all over the place. Unfortunately, it picks up a lot of little things, like jealousy, or overprotectiveness, or anger, or sadness, or simple nastiness. These negative energies clog up my radar. I can't just hear 'Murderer! Murderer!' loud and clear in my head. I wish I could."

Roxy sighed. "I wish you could too . . ."

Just then Dr. Jack came over. Roxy had heard a lot about him, interesting anecdotes, but she had never met him before. He was the owner of the botanica, the magical supplies store that she had visited a few times with Sage.

"Hello, Roxy."

"Dr. Jack, I'm so pleased to meet you. Thank you for closing up your botanica so you could attend this evening."

"Oh, I haven't closed it, my dear. My assistant, Leroy, is manning the fort. We have a commitment to stay open late. We are *always* open late." He leaned in conspiratorially.

"For the witches, the nocturnal ones, you know." He winked and tapped his nose.

Roxy broke into a smile. Dr. Jack was delightfully eccentric. He wore a rose pink felt fedora, mirrored sunglasses, and a purple leopard-print scarf. A royal-blue trench coat was draped over his trim body, and he wore a white shirt underneath a black velvet waistcoat and purple corduroy trousers. Simple black shoes completed the outfit.

"Did I just hear you two lovely ladies talking about justice?" he said, rubbing his short, gray beard. He spoke very softly.

"That you did," said Sage, smiling at him.

Roxy watched them both. The heart-shaped pink crystal popped back into her mind, and she mused how Dr. Jack and Sage would make an awesome couple.

"Justice is the most important topic facing us on this planet at present," he said. "Because we've rather failed on that front, haven't we? When one person can die of a preventable disease in childhood, and another can live in a luxurious mansion and go on to inherit huge wealth, all because of an accident of birth, it feels like we've gone wrong somewhere. An ovarian lottery of sorts, don't you think?" Dr. Jack looked at Roxy for confirmation.

Roxy nodded, a little stunned at the diversion the conversation had taken. Being around folks like Sage and Dr. Jack was like riding a roller coaster. From romance to murder, to witches, to justice, to privilege, you never knew what would pop up next! "You're right. Although Sage and I were really just talking about making sure Dash's killer is found." Then, feeling a little foolish, but also quite brave, she asked, "Do *you* have any means for finding out who could have killed him?"

"Spiritual technology to divine the identity of a killer?" he said. "This is not my specialty, I'm afraid."

Roxy felt she'd landed on another planet. *Spiritual technology? What was that?* But there was no time to ask as Evangeline and Nat came out with the cold canapés. This time, Roxy had successfully persuaded Evangeline to go along with her idea for "newfangled, posh fiddly stuff," and Evangeline had rather enjoyed making small versions of her crawfish pies, crab boulettes, and Cajun pork belly tacos. As she moved about the room, Nat's expression was inscrutable —she was *not* a believer in or fan of anything remotely magical. As far as she was concerned, crystal grids and spiritualism were mumbo-jumbo nonsense, but she knew better than to say so.

"Roxy!" Nat said. "You're not even dressed!" Nat had a trademark band tee on, but she had changed her boots. They were pink and matched the color printed on her T-shirt.

Roxy had gotten so caught up in the crystals and conversation that she'd forgotten to get ready. "Oh, my gosh!" she said.

Roxy dashed off to her room, fed Nefertiti, and dressed. She grinned as she pulled her outfit out of the wardrobe—a dress covered in gold sequins. She'd spotted it in a store near Sam's laundry but hadn't had occasion to wear it. It was a *very* bold choice. But what night could be better to debut it than an "Evening of Love and Light?"

She paired it with gold sparkling shoes, gold earrings, necklace and bangle, and a pearl bracelet. She even put a vine of golden flowers in her hair. Glittering from head to toe, she stepped back into the lounge. Predictably to everyone except Roxy, who was immune to her own beauty, all eyes turned to her. Some eyes, like Sam's, lingered.

"Wow, you look simply devastating!" Elijah said. He kissed her on both cheeks. Elijah was wearing a purple suit covered in green and blue skulls. It was quite the loudest outfit Roxy had ever seen.

"Thank you, you are too sweet," she said. "Now, I don't know about you, but I'm ready for some magic!"

Ada swept into the room looking as beautifully presented as usual. She was wearing a diaphanous tangerine gown that reached her ankles, and once again, her nails matched her outfit.

"Good evening!" Roxy said cheerfully.

Ada gave her a tight smile. "I am going out. I don't believe in crystals and those types of things. I came to New Orleans for the architecture, not some crazy, weirdo, woo-woo nonsense. It is incompatible with my spiritual beliefs."

"Okay, no problem!" Roxy said sunnily, clasping her hands tightly, determined that nothing would bring her down. "No problem at all. I hope you have a wonderful time."

Kathy, Dash's mother, on the other hand, was *not* so reluctant. She made a beeline for Sage's crystal table. Taking the glass of champagne Roxy offered her, she said, "Oh, I love all this stuff. Church on Sundays, psychic on Wednesdays, that's my routine." Ada sniffed and left.

Kathy's son Derek wasn't so keen on the evening's planned activities, either. As soon as he wandered into the room, he headed right out again, still playing with the model airplane he'd had when he'd arrived. "Bye," he mumbled, turning paler than ever when he saw what was laid out. As he left the room, Nefertiti, who had been sitting in the lobby, wandered lazily in. She jumped onto an armoire and parked herself down to watch the proceedings. Her eyes were alert, watchful.

"Derek's going to see Father John, the priest," Kathy said, her voice full of empathy. "He's struggling with . . . well, everything. I try to help him as best I can, but I'm struggling too. And there's only so much a momma can do. Besides, we're thinking of holding a celebration of life for Dash, something less formal than the memorial service. He's gone to talk arrangements with the priest." Roxy gave her a sympathetic smile.

Soon afterward, Sylvia and Lily came down together, deep in conversation about social media and their "conversion rates." They seemed to have become fast, if unlikely, friends and stood a little aloof from Kathy after nodding to her from the other side of the lounge. Michael hadn't yet shown up.

After he'd fixed the lights, Sam decided to stay for the evening. Crystals weren't really his thing, but he was open-minded and loved to learn about anything and everything, and as Roxy's friend, he wanted to support her as much as possible. Evangeline and Nat stayed out of sight in the kitchen mostly, Nat especially, although Evangeline could be seen peeking around the kitchen door from time to time, eager to view the scene.

And so the small crowd of Kathy, Sylvia, Lily, Sam, Elijah, Roxy, Sage, and Dr. Jack hung around drinking champagne, chatting, and admiring the crystals until Sage caught their attention.

CHAPTER TWENTY-TWO

"**W**HO WANTS A reading?" Sage said.

"Ooh, me please," said Sylvia immediately. She was clutching onto the frothy blue scarf wound around her neck, a point of elegance that elevated an otherwise bland outfit of beige button-down shirt and brown slacks. Roxy looked at her with new, appraising eyes. Sylvia had seemed more down-to-earth than this enthusiasm for crystals suggested. "I've never done anything like this before. Is it okay if I record it for my channel?" Sylvia added.

"Of course," said Sage. She paused and watched Sylvia for a moment as if she were reading her. "I warn you, though. It may get personal. Very personal."

"That's okay," Sylvia said. "My followers know just about everything about me anyway. I'm pretty much an open book."

The group sat down in the lounge. Sage and Sylvia sat in the center. Earlier, Roxy had arranged two chairs on either side of the coffee table for this very purpose. The atmosphere in the room became serious, and as they prepared themselves, a sense of gravity and purpose swept through the lounge like a draft.

Sage whipped a deck of tarot cards from a pocket in her robes and began to shuffle them. She closed her eyes. Nobody said a word as she concentrated. "I have a feeling we need to delve into the past, to bring something to light that needs to be cleared. Then, and only then, will the future be revealed."

Sylvia gulped. Her eyes flitted around the others sitting around the room. "Okay."

Roxy leaned forward. "Are you fine with doing this, Sylvia?"

Sylvia sat a little straighter in her seat. "Yes. Yes. It's no problem."

Sage spread the cards face down on the table in a long line. Dr. Jack hung back next to Roxy, looking on intently. He was the only one who remained standing. Roxy shivered. She sensed someone looking at her from behind and turned around. There was no one there. Dr. Jack caught her eye and raised one eyebrow.

"Choose three cards," Sage said, a heavy tone giving her already low voice even more gravitas.

Sylvia reached out tentatively and slid three cards toward her. Sage packed up the rest of the deck and slid it back into her pocket. She laid the three cards out in a row, still face down. With three quick flicks of her wrist, movements so swift everyone jumped, she turned them over.

Sage gasped. "The Three of Swords, a betrayal by a lover. The Justice card in reverse, meaning justice *not* served, and the Death card, meaning the end of something, or . . ."

Sylvia burst into tears. "Oh my goodness! This stuff really works!"

Kathy gave Roxy a triumphant nod. "If only that Ada was here to see this," she whispered.

Roxy didn't reply. Her heart had dropped. Now one of the influencers was crying. *And* she was recording! Roxy breathed in deeply and exhaled through her nose. There was nothing she could do so she kept smiling and clasped her hands together tightly in her lap. Her mind wandered to Michael. Where *was* he?

Sage leaned forward and took Sylvia's hands. "Let it out, my love. Let it out."

"I had a horrible, abusive ex-husband." She shuddered. "And I didn't leave him. Sometimes, I thought I deserved his abuse. Other times I knew I didn't, but was too afraid to leave." She wiped her tears and laughed. "Oh, I shouldn't get so emotional. It was twenty years ago now. A little more, in fact."

Sage nodded. "It's okay to cry. The wound is raw because something about it is not resolved. There is still a healing, still a message for you in this memory. What happened in the end?"

As though the intensity of the moment was too much for her, Sylvia sat back. She dropped Sage's hands and looked down into her lap.

"I finally found the strength, the courage to leave, and took off to Europe where he couldn't find me. I had no money. No home. I slept on couches, in hostels, even sometimes under railroad bridges. It wasn't easy. I felt like ending it all at times. But eventually I came back to the US, to a totally different state, and began my life over. I've never seen my ex-husband since."

Sage nodded slowly. "What is there left to release?"

"I . . . I don't know."

"Maybe there's a part of the story you haven't told?"

Sylvia looked bewildered. "Nothing that I can think of." She laughed, but to Roxy, it sounded a little forced. "Well, I won't underestimate a tarot reading in the future, that's for sure! I thought this was just going to be a little fun." She looked around at the others in the room, clearly hoping someone would rescue her. Her audience looked hesitant, a little awkward. Elijah was jiggling his foot vigorously. Sam rested his elbows on his knees looking very grave. Dr. Jack looked equally serious. Lily's expression was impassive, but she had turned her body away from the scene in the center and crossed her legs. Only Kathy looked eager, her eyes shining as she looked at Sylvia.

Roxy stepped in. "Perhaps that's enough of the cards for now? Maybe we could look at the crystals and talk about them."

"That's a good idea," said Lily Vashchenko in her slow, somber voice. She stood and pulled down her short cream skirt so that it hovered just above her knees and straightened her baby blue T-shirt. She walked over to the velvet-covered trestle table, her champagne glass in her hand. "I really like this one." She pointed to a crystal grid Sage had set up. "A grid is a configuration of crystals placed in a pattern that amplifies their intention. All crystals are infused with a purpose," Sage explained. "This grid comprises of peacock colored crystals—deep greens, blues, and purples. They represent healing and well-being."

"Isn't it lovely?" said Roxy, keen to raise the energy in the room.

"Hmm, I don't know." Kathy pointed at another grid full of oranges and yellow crystals. "This one is much more to my taste."

"Crystals are not just pretty colors," said Dr. Jack. "Though what you're drawn to *can* indicate personal issues you may be struggling with. They can also indicate what you're *comfortable* with." He pointed to Kathy's choice. "This one is for inviting cheerfulness and joy into your life. Or, conversely, you may be attracted to it if you use cheerfulness and joy *too* much, to cover up issues or hidden motivations, for instance."

Roxy felt distinctly awkward, and Kathy gave a laugh devoid of any kind of joy at all. She blinked at him and shook her head ever so slightly. "What on earth do you mean?"

Dr. Jack nodded. "Just like that."

CHAPTER TWENTY-THREE

"HUH?" KATHY SAID. She was still smiling, but now she looked like a shark baring its teeth. "In this society, we've become addicted to pleasure and afraid of what is uncomfortable," said Dr. Jack. "But the wise person knows that beyond discomfort and even downright pain lies truth. There are blessings and strength more than we could ever believe if we travel to journey's end."

This was all getting a little intense and complicated for Roxy. Her head was beginning to spin, and she got the impression that the evening wasn't going so well.

Sage turned to Lily. "Would you like a reading?"

Lily looked at her warily. "Oh, no, no, thank you. In fact, I have some fans in the area. I'm going to go and meet with them, actually. I'll be back later. See you!" With that, she was out the door. She didn't even bother with a jacket. Roxy felt a teeny-tiny bit like doing that herself.

Almost immediately there was a knock on the front door and in stepped Michael. "Sorry I'm late," he said. He looked a little more like his normal self than he had earlier, very serious, but he held his head high and made eye contact with everyone.

"Kathy," he said. He nodded politely in her direction.

"How nice to see you, Michael," she said, returning his gaze only briefly. She spoke like Evangeline's whiskey and caramel sauce was spread across her teeth.

Sage looked relieved to see him. "Michael, would *you* like a reading?"

"Absolutely," he said. His eyes lit up. "And I'd like to know more about these crystals."

Dr. Jack looked delighted. "I can answer all your questions."

"Awesome," Michael said briskly. He took his jacket off. "Let's do this."

Michael sat down for his reading. This time Roxy was unwilling to watch, it felt too intrusive, so she struck up a conversation with Sam.

"How's business going?" she asked.

"Ticking along nicely, as usual," he said.

"Ticking along?" said Roxy. "I didn't think you were a 'ticking along' sort of guy. I thought you were more about expansion and trying new things. That's what you've been encouraging me to do with the hotel all this time."

He gave a small smile, a little embarrassed. "Well, I *am* working on something."

"Do tell," Roxy said.

Sam rarely spoke about himself, his goals, his dreams. He seemed to prefer encouraging others. But now he said, "I'm thinking of setting up a program for the homeless."

"Wow," Roxy said. "That sounds bold."

"Yeah, I've been thinking about it for a while now. Sylvia was lucky. She had a way to come back from being down and out, but others aren't so fortunate. I'd like to offer a path for people who want to get back on their feet."

"And how would you do that?"

"I'd get them access to good healthcare, teach them skills so they can support themselves, employ them in my business to give them experience, and maybe build a network of other businesses for them to work in, that kind of thing."

"That *is* bold. Big and bold," said Roxy. "What a great idea! It could be massive."

"It should be relatively straightforward," he said. "I just have to . . ."

"Straightforward?" Roxy cried, astounded. It sounded complicated and overwhelming to her, but Sam had an easy, can-do, confident, nothing-was-too-difficult attitude. Who *was* this enigma? How did he get to be like that? And how could she become a little more like him?

"I should probably keep quiet about the idea for a bit," he said, "until it's up and running. I have so many ideas. If I talked about them all, I'd seem a huge flake. The vast majority never see the light of day." He laughed, his broad shoulders shaking a little. "So I keep my hands close to my chest until I know I can play winning cards."

"I wish I could do that," said Roxy. "I just tend to be a mess in front of everyone, and then it somehow works out. Or not."

"You don't look a mess in front of anyone."

"I worry about what people would say if I fail."

"Any undertaking involves risk, and risk requires courage. The only people who criticize others' failures are those who don't dare to take risks in the first place. They are not worth bothering with."

Roxy blinked. She hadn't thought of it that way before.

Sam was right. She felt a smidgeon of anxiety leave her, and she steepled her fingers in front of her. She might have grown an inch or so. She certainly felt happier.

Elijah sidled over to them. "Look, Rox. Have you considered speaking to those awful reporters outside? I know there's not many of them left, and the Lord knows when we were teeming with them, they drank so much coffee and ate so many of my pastries they increased my bottom line no end, but the stragglers are bothering my regulars. They're costing me business." He winced. "I thought that perhaps if you spoke to them they might go away."

"Yeah, I think you should, Roxy," Sam said. He caught sight of the look Roxy gave him. She might be small and not so brave at times, but she didn't like being *told* what to do. He raised his hands. "Okay, okay, give it some thought. Just say something, not much, a short statement, just enough for them to be pacified. It doesn't help anyone, them being on your doorstep all day."

Roxy folded her arms. She did *not* want to do that.

Sam looked over at Michael. The influencer was engrossed in conversation with Dr. Jack and Sage. "He looks all right, thank goodness."

Roxy wanted to talk to Michael and find out how he was doing—she felt a sort of duty of care toward him—but he was in the midst of what appeared to be an animated discussion. Michael was gesticulating excessively, but his expression was warm. He was enjoying himself. She knew that with Sage and Dr. Jack, Michael would be fine. "He's in good hands," she said.

Sam smiled at her. "Indeed. Even if they are a little eccentric."

Roxy laughed quietly. "Just a little."

CHAPTER TWENTY-FOUR

THE EARLY MORNING sun poured into Roxy's room and she woke up with a newfound sense of joy. She felt utterly refreshed. It was as if the good energy from the crystals the previous evening had swept away all her cares and worries, leaving confidence and optimism in their place. Nefertiti was sleeping beside her, and Roxy sunk her hands into her soft white fur. The cat woke and blinked at her. She looked as if she might be smiling too.

"Good morning, princess," Roxy said. "How are you this morning?"

"Meeeooowwww."

Roxy giggled. "Right! I have the feeling that today is going to be a good day."

Her mood didn't even dip when she thought of Dash. She remembered what Sage had said—that Dash was on the other side, watching them. She knew that Michael would honor Dash's memory in only the best ways and that Dash's message of the importance of realizing one's dreams would be spread far and wide.

They still hadn't heard from the police beyond the initial interviews. Detective Johnson had been very tight-lipped. She didn't know how the investigation was going or what kind of poison had killed Dash, nor did she know how it had gotten into his bloodstream. All of them in the hotel that night were under suspicion for murder, and there was the still unresolved question of the role her hotel's food had played in Dash's death. The forensics team had returned just like Johnson had promised they would. They had taken away samples of food from the kitchen, but Roxy had heard nothing. Even if it were found that her food had nothing to do with Dash's death, Roxy knew as well as anyone that mud stuck. But even that didn't matter right then. The sense of calm that pervaded her was too deep to feel any sort of worry at all. Everything would work out. Of course, it would.

After showering and dressing in a canary yellow sundress—something she only felt good wearing when she was feeling just as sunny inside—Roxy headed to the kitchen. There was a wonderful aroma coming from it.

"Morning, Nat!" Roxy said, cheerfully.

Evangeline wasn't working that morning. Nat had got the hang of making all the breakfast dishes now, and Evangeline liked her lie-ins.

Nat flashed her a grin, looking back from the big pot she was stirring. "Hey, girl."

"I feel wonderful this morning," Roxy said. "Like everything's going to work out. I feel like maybe taking Sylvia and Lily and the rest of them on some kind of tour. A boat trip, maybe?"

"Great idea!" said Nat. "I'd like to come too. I think we could all do with a nice little cocktail cruise to forget our troubles."

"Cocktails! You're a genius!" said Roxy. "That sounds like just the remedy. The influencers will be able to take wonderful pictures down the river too."

Nat nodded. "Glad I could help."

Roxy grinned mischievously. "So how did you like the tarot reading and crystals last night?" She chuckled. "Get any messages from the other side?" Nat was *not* into anything spiritual or magical, and Roxy enjoyed teasing her about it.

"Of course not!" Nat said. "I hid in the kitchen all evening, didn't I? Load of rubbish." There was a little pause before she said sheepishly, "But I *do* have to say that I woke up feeling fantastic."

"Me *too*!" said Roxy. "It's like . . . I don't know, it's hard to describe. Maybe like . . . like the air has glitter in it!"

Nat burst out laughing. "You crazy, girl, but I know exactly what you mean! I got up all excited. Got everything ready so everyone can have a full cooked breakfast if they want one. *And* I've been for a run." Nat lived in a unit that was situated immediately behind the Funky Cat. "But of course, that has *nothing* to do with *crystals*."

Roxy grinned. "No, nothing at all."

"How about Dr. Jack, though?" Nat said excitedly. "He's so wonderfully nuts. When do you think we'll be invited to his and Sage's wedding?"

"That's what I was thinking!" said Roxy. "He's exactly her type. They'd be wonderful together."

"Totally! And then Sage would be able to *live* in a magical supplies store. Wouldn't that be her dream? He told me he lives in the apartment above it."

"She would be in heaven," Roxy said. She let out a happy sigh. "I love living here. Don't you?"

"Yep," said Nat. "And it looks like Detective Johnson

isn't focused on me at all, so that's a plus. I am always really worried around him, but he's not said anything to me about, you know, *my paperwork*. I guess he hasn't noticed, or maybe he doesn't care. Perhaps murder investigations are his one and only thing. Anything beyond that, and he's not interested."

"Probably," said Roxy. "He does seem very focused. Laser-like. He hasn't contacted us with any update though, has he?"

Nat laughed. "Thank goodness. No news is good news."

"Are you going to do anything about your status?" Roxy asked, quietly. "Try to get legal?"

Nat bit her lip. "Well, to be honest, Rox, Sam told me that if I was found out, *you* could be in trouble too. You know, for hiring me, so I'm going to do something about it. It's not fair to you for me to stick my head in the sand. I'll get it sorted out, I promise. Sam said he'd help."

"I'm sure it will be okay. Can't you find yourself a handsome Southern gentleman to make an honest woman of you?"

"Oh! Perhaps that's what Sam meant! Me and Sam, can you imagine?" Nat threw her head back and laughed.

Once again, Roxy felt a little ripple of defensiveness at the mention of Sam. "You need to get out there and mingle, girlfriend."

"Ugh." Nat laughed and shuddered. "I *hate* that word. Mingle."

Roxy chuckled. "You make me laugh."

"Hello?" someone called from the dining room.

Roxy hurried out to see Sylvia. "Hi there, Sylvia, good morning. How did you sleep?"

"Great, thank you!" Sylvia said. "I feel so rested. I was just wondering if breakfast had started yet."

"Nope, but it can start just for you," said Roxy, gesturing at the table. "Both Nat and I were saying how well we slept too. It sounds a little woo, but I'm wondering if it isn't the energy of the crystals doing their thing."

Sylvia sat down. "It really could be. Sage certainly cut right to the chase with me!"

"Indeed, she did," said Roxy. "I hope the reading wasn't too uncomfortable for you."

"Well, it was at the time," said Sylvia. "But sometimes it's good to be uncomfortable. I feel renewed and happy now."

Roxy smiled. "I'm so glad to hear it. Now, tell me, what would you like for breakfast? We can do just about anything you want. The full works, if you like, or beignets that are up-to-the-minute fresh."

"Ooh, what about bacon and eggs?" Sylvia said.

"Coming right up!" said Roxy. "Why not have them with a New Orleans twist—eggs deviled with Cajun spice, and praline bacon?"

"Yum. Sounds wonderful!" Sylvia said.

Roxy dashed into the kitchen to give Nat Sylvia's order, then came back out to chat with the influencer while she waited.

"So how have you enjoyed your time with us so far?" Roxy said. "I know, of course, with . . . Dash, it's not quite the same. But I hope you're still getting something out of your trip."

"Oh, yes," said Sylvia. "It is tragic about that young man. He was so young, with so much life to live. And I feel for Michael and Kathy and Derek so much. I'm praying for their healing." With a sad expression, Sylvia looked down at her fingers on the tablecloth. Roxy noticed they were a little gnarled with arthritis. Sylvia lifted her head before resuming. "This is the first time I've been to New Orleans. While I love your hotel, especially the staff and food, I'd love to get out and see more of the city. I need to take more photos and videos for my Instagram account. My followers are like greedy children. They need feeding every couple of hours."

"How about we all take a cruise down the river? Nat and I were just talking about it. How does that sound?"

"Fabulous," said Sylvia, smiling. "I'm looking forward to it already."

CHAPTER TWENTY-FIVE

THE FEELING THAT everything was going to be just fine continued as everyone came down for breakfast. Lily Vashchenko glided down the staircase with a smile while Ada was a little kinder than usual. She even asked Sylvia how the previous evening had gone. Derek was, as always, extremely quiet and shy, but Kathy took care of him. She helped him order a huge breakfast of bacon, eggs, sausages, beans, rice, and French toast. Everyone marveled at how he stayed so thin.

"We're planning on a cruise down the Mississippi later. Is everyone up for that?" Roxy asked. They all nodded in agreement.

"Dash loved the water," said Kathy.

Roxy leaned over and gave her a hug. "You sound so incredibly strong, Kathy."

The older woman held her head high. "Dash would have wanted me to be. I can hear his voice now. *'Don't worry about it, Mom!'* he'd say. He always said that. I'm trying to channel his spirit instead of being a ball of anxiety. I want to be like him, fearless and brave."

Later that morning, they headed out for the boat ride. Roxy called Michael at his hotel to see if he would come along, but there was no answer. A few reporters still hung around the steps outside, so a plan was hatched to avoid them. Three of them acted as decoy and went out the front door. Once they saw Nat, Sylvia, and Derek emerge from the Funky Cat, the reporters immediately ignored them and returned to distractedly scrolling endlessly on their phones while the more newsworthy quarry of Roxy, Lily, and Kathy escaped via the back. They met up on the street at the end of the alleyway. The group walked along the streets of New Orleans together in a gaggle beneath a bright sun. The sky was a wonderful, creamy blue. It was a beautiful day for a cruise.

"Some of the best boat rides go from the French Quarter," Nat said. "Let's head in that direction."

So they did and found themselves a glorious steamer. The captain was standing around on the riverfront, looking bored. He looked as though he had been there a while, and no one was interested in what he had to offer. Monday mornings were pretty quiet.

It was a *very* large boat—named Marie—and far too large for their small party. Roxy guessed 200 people could have fit onto it. But there was no one else around. Nat barreled her way to the front of their group and demonstrated to them, and the captain, her negotiating chops. They had been honed in the flea markets of New Orleans. Nat skillfully persuaded the captain to allow them to commandeer the entire boat for just a small fee so that they could leave immediately and keep their party private. Roxy knew she was getting an amazing bargain, and with a nod to Nat, produced her credit card before the man could change his mind.

"Where's the bartender?" Lily asked when they got on board.

"It's Monday. It's her day off," the captain growled.

As one, their faces fell. Their disappointment was total. They had been looking forward to their cocktails.

"No problem! I can do it. Before Instagram came along, I supported my travels with bartending. That's how I got started in this biz." They all turned to look at Sylvia, a gray-haired, cargo-panted, slightly arthritic, sixty-something woman, in surprise and not a little respect. "If I can have access to the bar, I can make us all cocktails."

Seven pairs of eyes immediately swiveled to the steamer's captain. After a few moments pause during which he surveyed their eager expressions as he considered Sylvia's request, he reached for a huge bunch of keys, one of which unlocked the bar. Sylvia immediately got to work cleaning glasses and checking the stock.

"It's a bit early for me," Roxy said when she saw Sylvia reach for some brandy. It was only 11 o'clock.

"Don't you worry, my dear, mocktails are my specialty. I'll rustle up something delicious you'll love."

Soon they were out on the open water, cocktails and mocktails in hand.

Roxy stood nearby the captain in the pilothouse. "So, why *Marie*?"

"After Marie Laveau, of course!" The boat's captain wasn't particularly polite and certainly not gracious. "Rough around the edges," Nat would have called him.

"Who's Marie Laveau?"

"Only the Voodoo Queen of New Orleans!" he said. "Her mausoleum is in the Saint Louis cemetery. You haven't heard of it?" He looked at her incredulously.

"People still go to her grave and ask her to grant them their wishes."

"Huh," Roxy said.

"You have to mark an X on the grave, turn around three times, then yell out your wish. If it's granted, you're to come back, draw a circle around the X, and leave her an offering as thanks," the captain continued. "If you don't, well, you know . . ." He raised his eyebrows as high as they would go.

Just a few months ago, faced with a comment like that, Roxy would have felt as though she'd entered a different world. Now that she was steeped in the mysticism of the city, she didn't blink an eye. "Oh, I'll have to visit," she said mildly.

The cruise was delightful. Jazz music wafted through the speakers, making it all the more relaxing. Nat got everyone tapping their feet and swaying as she sang along to the upbeat *Hit the Road, Jack* and the more soulful *Cry Me a River*. They got wonderful views of the city as they cruised by, and Lily and Ada and Sylvia took so many pictures and videos, that Roxy marveled at the full-time job it must be to sort out which shots would make it onto their social media accounts.

The cruise went on for a little over three hours, and thanks to Sylvia, the cocktails were colorful and became more intense (alcoholic) as the journey went on. By the time they cruised back to the dock they'd launched from, the whole party was playful and in high spirits. Even Derek had come out of his shell a little and was trotting up and down the top deck while his mother, frightened that he might fall in the water, told him to calm down. The group felt closer, somehow, like the water running beneath them had bonded them together.

"Great idea you had, Nat," Roxy said, as the boat

cruised back to dock. Roxy felt relaxed for the first time in days.

"What?" Nat sat on a bench looking out from the side of the boat, her eyes closed, the gentle breeze from across the river making strands of her bobbed hair dance.

"This cruise, it was a great idea. Got us all out in the fresh air. We needed it." Roxy caught sight of a man standing on the riverside. "Oh no. Really? Now?"

"What?" Nat repeated.

"It's him."

"Who?" Nat stood and turned. She shielded her eyes from the sun as she looked toward the dock they had left from. Standing there waiting for their return was Detective Johnson.

Roxy disembarked first. She felt it was her duty as the owner of the hotel and organizer of the trip.

"Come here," Johnson ordered, as soon as she stepped off the boat. Roxy bristled. This felt like a very hard reintroduction to the reality of life on the ground after their relaxing cruise on the water. Johnson held his hand up to the others who were readying to leave the paddleboat. "Ms. Reinhardt only. Everyone else must wait."

Roxy's heart thudded in her chest as Johnson led her away.

"What's wrong?" Roxy said.

"Michael O'Sullivan was attacked last night. Beaten up and left unconscious. He was on the way back from an evening at your hotel, I understand." Johnson looked at her. He squinted, deliberately lowering his head to study her.

"Oh, my gosh! Is he okay?"

"Yes, he is. He went to the hospital for some treatment and is now being monitored for a concussion, but he'll be fine. I need all your guests to come to the station for questioning. I have squad cars standing by the curb. You need to explain to them all what's going on."

"Do you . . . do you think it has anything to do with Dash's death?"

"I don't know. Probably."

Roxy closed her eyes in despair. What had she gotten these people *into*? And which one of them was a murderer?

CHAPTER TWENTY-SIX

I F ROXY HAD felt like a billion dollars when stepping out of the Funky Cat earlier that day, she felt like less than a dime coming back in. It was still only late afternoon, but it felt like so much time had passed, it should have been late at night. Before they left the police station, Johnson had assembled the group in the lobby. Roxy, Nat, Kathy, Derek, Sylvia, Lily, and Ada stood before him. Various expressions of anger, boredom, and exhaustion stared back at him. "Now, you are all free to go, but I will be keeping an eye on you. No one must leave the city, and," he glared at Roxy, "no meddling, d'ya hear me?" The group nodded and, grumbling just a little, turned to trudge their way out of the station and back to the Funky Cat.

"Well, we are certainly seeing the sights of New Orleans today," Sylvia said cheerily. "Now we've seen the inside of the local police station!" Roxy closed her eyes momentarily. Could this Instagram promotion campaign get any worse?

When they arrived back at the hotel, Roxy and Nat headed straight for the kitchen to make po' boy sandwiches.

They were all ravenous. It was in the kitchen that they found Sage. She was wired. Roxy had come to know this was Sage's "business" energy. When she was coding for her clients or working on the marketing for the Funky Cat, she was as sharp as a razor. She buzzed around getting things done at the speed of light. It was such a clear distinction from her usual, peaceful, floating energy and unquestionably, wordlessly telegraphed what she was doing.

Sage was munching on a beignet while tapping furiously away on her laptop with the other hand. "Client's got a major issue," she said through a mouthful. "I'm going to be gone for the rest of the day. You don't need me for anything, do you?"

Roxy *did* need her. There was something so reassuring about having Sage around. The African-American woman felt like an ever-loving mother figure who could comfort Roxy and make her feel safe. But Roxy didn't know how to say that. Plus, she was the proprietor of a hotel. She needed to be strong. An adult. "No problem," Roxy said with a forced smile. "Go ahead. We'll be fine."

"Do you know what happened?" Nat asked Sage.

"No . . . what?" Nat explained what had happened to Michael.

Sage frowned. "But Dr. Jack and Michael walked back together from here last night. How could that have happened?"

"Apparently they separated at some point and Michael walked on to the Hyatt alone," Roxy said. "That's when he was attacked, according to Detective Johnson."

"Oh," said Sage. "What *is* going on right now? The energies are very, *very* strange at the moment. Up and down, up and down, up and down, and all over the place."

"I'll say," said Roxy.

"Well, I really must be going," said Sage. "I'm so sorry, I know this isn't a good time for me to jump ship, but I'll send healing energy through the building and into the air so that you will all feel more grounded and at peace."

Roxy smiled, not knowing if Sage was amazing or absolutely crazy.

Sage paused for a moment, closed her eyes, and waved her hands back and forth. Then she said a quick, "Goodbye! I leave you in love!" and was gone.

Nat and Roxy continued to make po' boys in silence. The atmosphere in the kitchen was a little lighter, but still quite somber. Nat turned on Evangeline's old-fashioned radio, and it crackled into life. The station played authentic Deep South jazz music, and the sounds of a double bass solo bubbled into the room, bringing some warmth with it.

After being grilled by Detective Johnson, no one was feeling particularly sociable, so Roxy and Nat took the roast beef po' boys, chips, and salad to the guests' rooms and returned to the dining room, where they sat down to eat. Roxy poured herself some coffee and offered Nat a cup. Nat shook her head.

"So who *wasn't* here last night when Michael and Dr. Jack left?" Roxy mused.

"Well, Ada left earlier so she wasn't here at all," said Nat. "I think we need to keep a proper eye on *her*."

"Yes, I know you don't like her," Roxy said, a little more sharply than she meant to. "But I don't see a real motive for harming Michael, let alone killing Dash."

"Oh, come on. Dash *humiliated* her."

"I don't think she'd kill for that," said Roxy. "Anyway, I think it's much more likely to be Lily. She wants to win the Hilton Hotels sponsorship, and Michael and Dash were after it too. Imagine if she took Dash out, and then last night she tried to stop Michael?" Roxy's heart skipped a beat. "Remember, she ducked out when Sage offered to do a reading for her? She said she was going out to see her fans. I didn't see what time she came back in. Did you?"

"No," said Nat. "But it can't be her. She's so elegant and fine!"

"I think she has the strongest motive so far," said Roxy. "*And* she doesn't have good alibis. She was in the hotel the night Dash was killed and she was missing for part of last night too.

"Perhaps we can get in contact with the fans she saw," said Nat, "and find out the time she was with them."

Roxy sighed. "Johnson warned me off investigating right when Dash's body was found, and you heard him in the lobby of the station earlier. We're not supposed to investigate at all. We shouldn't even be talking about it. I mean what are we thinking? We're discussing which of our guests could be a murderer! Let's talk about something else, get our minds off it."

CHAPTER TWENTY-SEVEN

SO NAT TOLD Roxy all about the next pair of Doc Martens she planned to buy. "They have a white skull and red roses design and come with bright red ribbon laces that look just *awesome* when tied in a bow." Then Nat explained how she was going to upcycle the new table and sculpture they'd bought on their trip to the flea market and that a niche goth band she liked would be in town later in the month. "Could I have an evening off to go see them?"

"Of course," Roxy said.

"Thank you. And now, I'm going to prep some vegetables in case anyone wants dinner later," Nat announced.

Roxy got up from the table and stretched. "I feel so tired," she said. "Like all the energy's been sucked out of me."

Nat smiled wryly. "Being around Johnson will do that to a girl, right?"

Roxy sighed. "Unfortunately, yes."

"Go have a nap."

"I can't," said Roxy. "I have some admin stuff to do, and

I also need to decide if I should speak to these darn reporters that are still hanging around. Elijah's saying they are affecting his business. His regulars aren't coming around so often because they are bothered by the reporters. He asked if I'd consider speaking to them. It might get them to go away, he said, but I'm not convinced. Sam agreed with him."

"Yeah, but they've faded away now, pretty much," Nat said. "There's just a few left. It's not like it was before. We didn't even have any follow us when we went for the boat ride, did we?"

"That's because we were clever," said Roxy. "Still, it might be the proper thing for me to make some kind of statement. What do you think?"

Nat shrugged. "I have no idea, Rox. Just do what you want to do, I say." She put their plates into the dishwasher. "See you later!" she called as Roxy picked up her coffee and headed to the tiny little office that was next to her bedroom. "I'll be back in time to help you with dinner," Roxy replied.

Roxy's office had once been a much larger space, but it was rarely used and had become a dumping ground for all sorts of items that "might come in useful someday." The room had been filled with spare crockery, a broken washing machine, and bed linen that no one ever used. Papers from as far back as the 1980s had been strewn next to electrical parts that no one knew what to do with. There had even been a bicycle wheel propped up against the wall. During the refurbishment, the junk had been cleared out, and walls were put up to divide the space into a new, sleek office on one side, and Roxy's personal rooms on the other.

The office was absolutely tiny, but Roxy *adored* it. It had a large window looking out onto the cobbled street, and she'd painted the walls one of her favorite colors, aquamarine. She had a brilliant white desk, a slimline white laptop, a white spinning chair that Nat had painted to make look distressed, and a glossy white table lamp. The dark wooden floorboards had been polished until they shined, and everything felt *just right*.

Roxy used a computer to do the hotel accounts. Sage had taught her how, but she still wrote them down in a book too. The physical act of writing out the numbers made her feel more in touch with the financial health of the business than did tapping keys and moving a mouse around. She used an aquamarine gel pen—she had quite a few of them, all kept in a sparkly green box—and wrote everything down in a navy blue ledger.

Roxy spent a little time filling it in and balancing the petty cash. She put on some relaxing music, checked her email, and updated the hotel's Facebook and Instagram pages. Before she realized it, two hours had flown by. Hearing Nat clattering around in the dining room as she laid tables for dinner caused her to pay attention to the time. Roxy looked at her watch, astounded, then got up and stretched her neck from side to side. Where *had* the time gone?

She left her office and noiselessly walked into the kitchen. She made Nat jump. "Oh gosh, you scared me!" Nat cried.

"Hey," Roxy said, blinking. She felt like she was waking from a dream. "Sorry about that. I got into some kind of zone, a business accounts and petty cash zone if you can believe that. I've literally had my head down since I last saw you. And not for a nap." She raised the cup of coffee she was still nursing, the coffee long cold.

"Rather you than me. Look, I'm going to have a fifteen-minute rest before I start dinner," Nat said.

"I think I'll do the same," said Roxy. "See you in a few."

Roxy opened the door to her room and straight away looked around for Nefertiti. Her little cat seemed to love staying in her room even though she had the freedom to roam just about wherever she liked in the hotel. It was certainly quiet and peaceful for her in there but not very interesting. Still, Nefertiti seemed to be perfectly content most of the time. Occasionally, when the sun was shining, the Persian would meow to be let out and sun herself in the courtyard, looking nothing short of regal. But now, Nefertiti was curled up on Roxy's chair, purring in her sleep. Roxy took off her shoes and gave her cat a tickle under her chin. It was only then that she noticed something by the door, a slip of paper on the floor. She'd stepped over it when she came in. Roxy bent to pick it up, frowning.

> *LOOK INTO SYLVIA'S STORY. YOU'RE ONLY
> GETTING HALF THE PICTURE.*

It was written in capital letters. The handwriting was shaky like the person was writing with their opposite hand or they were trembling. The paper was unlined and smartly folded.

Roxy walked back to her bed slowly, reading the note again. Was it genuine? Or was it malicious? And who could have left it?

Now Roxy was *wide* awake and the possibility of a rest was gone. She climbed onto her bed and reached for her phone.

She navigated to the browser and typed "Sylvia Walters" into the search bar. All she saw was a list of Facebook profiles for women with the same name, none of them the Sylvia that she knew. Roxy tried again.

"Sylvia Walters' story"

"The truth about Sylvia Walters"

"Sylvia Walters' scam"

All of these search terms turned up nothing at all. It was only when she searched "Sylvia Walters' secret" that Roxy came across something, and even that was buried deep, deep in the search results. On page fourteen, in fact.

CHAPTER TWENTY-EIGHT

T HE MUSINGS OF a Middle-Aged, Mid-Western Mom.

The blog didn't look very professional at all—more like a site made from a free template. The second to last entry was dated 10 years ago.

But the last post, the most recent one, the one that when she read it had Roxy's breath catching in her chest, was from just one year ago. Obviously, the blog owner had given up on broadcasting their thoughts to the world but had deemed this subject worthy of logging back in after a nine-year break.

The secrets you don't know about popular Instagram influencer Sylvia Walters.

Roxy scanned the article quickly, her eyes darting from side to side across her phone screen. The blogger wrote that she was from Sylvia's hometown, a place with a population of less than 5,000 in Illinois but wasn't specific.

> *But Sylvia Walters isn't even her real*
> *name. It's Helen Matheson. Don't believe*
> *me?*

There was a grainy photo of the front page of a newspaper—an image of a woman, her hands cuffed, walking out of court surrounded by police officers. The headline screamed:

KILLER WIFE TRIAL CONTINUES!

Roxy thought her heart might burst out of her chest. Killer wife? She squinted at the newspaper photo, but it was hard to see if it really was Sylvia. The woman in the picture looked larger, but Roxy supposed Sylvia might have lost weight since then. She read through what the "Middle-Aged Mom" had to say.

Well-known Instagram influencer, Sylvia
Walters AKA Helen Matheson, was sentenced
to 20 years in prison for killing her
husband Raymond Matheson in an altercation
at their home. When she was released, she
took a new name and moved to a new state.

I had forgotten all about her until I saw
her posts in my Instagram feed. I recognized
her immediately and saw that she had written
a book. I bought it. It is packed with LIES.

In it, Sylvia/Helen says she spent a
lengthy time in Europe, but I'm writing to

tell you that she was never in Europe. She was in JAIL. For killing her husband. The jury found that her attack on him was NOT in reasonable self-defense.

Raymond Matheson was a good man and well-loved by his community. Sylvia/Helen's defense was that he was abusing her, but no one in our town believes that. We think she was trying to kill him for the insurance money but got caught before she could cash in. Anyone who comes into contact with this so-called "Sylvia Walters" should BEWARE. She is a liar and a convicted felon. Steer clear!

Roxy put her phone down on the bed. This was all too weird for words. Was it true? But why would anyone make it up?

Roxy's thoughts were whizzing through her brain far too fast. All of a sudden her bedroom was too small. The walls felt like they were closing in on her. Her head was hurting. She needed coffee and she had an overwhelming urge to get out of the hotel.

Roxy slipped her shoes back on, squeezed out a pouch of cat food into Nefertiti's bowl, and headed out of her room, grabbing her coffee cup as she did so. It was in the lobby that she bumped into none other than Sylvia. She was carrying her trekking poles. Roxy gasped.

"You look like you've seen a ghost!" said Sylvia, laughing. "I don't look *that* bad in a tracksuit, do I?"

"Oh no, not at all!" Roxy said. "I just didn't expect

anyone to be here. It's been quite a day. I'm a bit on edge, that's all."

Sylvia pursed her lips and nodded. "I know what you mean. It has been a day." Sylvia looked at Roxy's cup. "You know, I gave up coffee a while back to manage my stress. It's helped tremendously," she said. "Nothing after 2 PM, otherwise I get these anxious thoughts at evening time. I thought I actually suffered from anxiety and went to the doctor for medication, but before I took any, someone suggested I give up caffeine as an experiment. I've been anxiety-free ever since! You should try it."

At any other time, this would have been very interesting to Roxy, but right now Sylvia's prattling made her want to scream. Maybe in the future, she *would* give up caffeine, but for now, she just needed to be alone to *think*.

"I'm going to try that," Roxy said, pointing her finger in the air. "Maybe I'll get some decaf in the meantime."

"Good idea," said Sylvia. "I'm going for my power walk now, down by the riverside. I'll be back in time for dinner. Want to come?"

"No, no. You go. Have fun," said Roxy.

Sylvia smiled. She waved. "See you!"

Roxy whipped out her phone and pulled up the city library website. After scrolling around the site, she texted Nat.

Sorry, can't help with dinner after all.
Have to go do something. I found out
something crazy. Talk later.

Roxy put her coffee cup behind the reception table and headed out the door, not even sure in what direction she was headed. She consulted her phone for the street name and punched it into her maps app.

Roxy ran to her destination. Unable to stop herself, she sprinted so fast she could hear the wind rushing past her ears. She only slowed to a jog when her destination came into view.

The library was housed in a huge colonial mansion fronted with white pillars and white woodwork. Out of breath, Roxy slowed her pace to a walk. As her heart rate slowed, she also started to doubt herself again. What had seemed like a no-brainer back at the Funky Cat—delve into the library records—now felt like an over-reaction.

Still, over the past few months, Roxy had gotten a lot better at trusting her intuition. She marched into the library and up to the librarian's desk. "Hi there, good evening," she said breathlessly. "I was wondering if you have a way of looking up old newspaper content. Say from 20 years ago?"

"Sure we do," said the librarian, a kindly looking man in his 60s. "A New Orleans paper?"

"Well, no. Illinois. But I'm not sure *where* in Illinois."

The man grimaced. "Might have a problem there. What information are you looking for?"

"I want to look up reporting about a woman. A Helen Matheson. She was on trial for murder."

"Okay," the man said as if this were a perfectly normal request. "Come over here to this computer, and we'll access the database."

An hour later, Roxy walked out of the library, shivers running up and down her spine. It could have been because she was still only wearing her yellow sundress and the sun was going down, but more likely it was because she *had* located Helen Matheson in the online database. Everything the blog had said was true. Roxy had even seen a picture. Helen Matheson was clearly and indisputably a younger version of the woman she knew as silver-haired, sexagenarian Sylvia Walters.

Roxy meandered through backstreets on her way home, her thoughts mirroring her rambling walk. She was so distracted, she found herself by the river without even knowing how she got there. Chewing her lip, she sat down on a bench and thought some more. If anyone could see inside her brain, they would have seen ideas and theories shooting between her synapses, like spectacular lightning bolts exploding in an electric storm.

She didn't want to go back to the hotel just yet. How would she face Sylvia with all these questions in her head? Roxy had always been great at hiding her feelings, but *only* if she was quiet and could make herself small, practically invisible. She used to be able to do that without too much effort, but now? Now, she had to be an upbeat, welcoming host who constantly ministered to her guests. Hiding her emotions in the type of situation she now found herself felt almost impossible. She was too honest.

When Roxy came to the small cobbled street that led to the Funky Cat, she walked right past it. She wasn't ready to go home just yet. She would visit Sam at his laundry. There were still a couple of reporter's vans parked on the street near the inn, but she strode along, confident that the journalists wouldn't notice her as long as she walked purposefully.

But Roxy's confidence was misplaced. As she turned a corner, she bumped into a female reporter. The other woman had been walking quickly and banged into Roxy with some force. Thick black hair tumbled in waves over the reporter's shoulders, and she struggled to move freely in her tight black skirt suit and high heels. Roxy didn't recognize her and wouldn't have known she was a reporter by sight, but for the microphone that the woman wielded like a weapon in front of her bright red lips.

The woman stumbled back, shocked for a moment but recovered in an instant. "Roxy Reinhardt!" she cried.

...as you would have known that she was not wearing clothes
but for the suggestion that the woman thanked him a
...shion in front of her bright red lips.
The woman troubled him. She called it a moment he
recovered in an instant. "Yes," he answered, he said.

CHAPTER TWENTY-NINE

"ROXY REINHARDT, THE manager of the Funky Cat Inn, formerly a call center operator with Modal Appliances, Inc. My name is Mariah Morales, KQNR-20 Nightly News." The woman assumed an expression of concern. "Tell me, Roxy, a murder was previously connected to your establishment when owned by Evangeline Smith. How do you explain this second death? A poisoning at that." She shoved the microphone in Roxy's face, awaiting answers to her questions, and gestured urgently toward a man with a camera. "Come on, Sheldon!" Morales hissed.

Roxy felt a huge lump rise in her throat. The microphone terrified her, and she felt adrenaline shoot through her body as, like a cornered animal, she looked for an escape route. "Sorry, I can't say anything," she gasped. A car passed and seeing Morales' microphone, the driver honked the car's horn loudly. The sound startled the reporter and for a second she took her eyes off Roxy. Seizing her opportunity, Roxy fled, hoping Mariah couldn't follow in her stiletto heels.

Propelled by a speed that she didn't know she possessed, Roxy flew down side streets and across sidewalks. People scattered to let her through. Shame burned in Roxy's pink cheeks, but her feet drove her forward and away from Mariah Morales and her menacing microphone. Why, oh *why* hadn't she been content living her quiet little life? Why had she chosen to live bigger? Why couldn't she have enjoyed the total obscurity of being a call center operator?

By the time she exploded through Sam's doorway, Roxy was angry with herself, with the world, and especially with Mariah Morales. She found Sam at the front desk, quietly doing some paperwork. He raised his head in surprise when she shot through the door.

"I'm so *sick* of this!" she burst out.

Sam laughed a little. "Hello to you too, Roxy."

"Sorry," she said, glaring at him. She looked back to see if Mariah and her cameraman Sheldon had followed her. They had. She could see Morales tottering on her high heels up the street, Sheldon jogging beside her.

"Help! The press. They're following me."

"Here." Sam parted a rack of shirts each draped in plastic. "Behind there. Be still. Don't make a noise."

Roxy slipped in between the shirts, and Sam let them fall so that they obscured her.

Mariah pushed open the door to the laundry and said, "Can I just . . .?"

"I'm sorry, no, you can't," Sam said walking up to her.

"But . . ."

"This is private property, and I ask that you remove yourselves immediately."

Mariah stretched her red lips into an especially beguiling smile. "I can assure you, sir, that we . . ."

"No," Sam said firmly, not swayed by her feminine wiles, attractive as they were. "Please leave right now. That is all. You are trespassing."

Mariah's expression quickly changed into a scowl. "Whatever." She flounced out, carelessly allowing the door to close on Sheldon who scurried behind her, the big camera he carried on his shoulder weighing him down.

Sam locked the door behind them. "You can come out now, Roxy." There was a rustle of plastic as the shirts parted and Roxy appeared, red-faced and windswept. "The reporters are still bothering you, I see," he said.

"Yes," said Roxy. "You saved me. Thank you. I don't know what came over me, I just ran and ran." She was feeling a little better already. The laundry was lovely and warm, and the thrum of the machines was hypnotic. They relaxed her. She flopped down on a plastic chair. She felt safe here with Sam.

"But the reporter is not really what's on my mind."

"So what's up?" he said.

"I found out some things about one of my guests. She's not been truthful, and I'm not sure what to do. Not in the circumstances. I'd like your help, your advice."

"You don't seem to like it when I give you advice. So I don't know how I can help."

"This time it's different, I'm *asking* for your advice—about this little . . . um, *investigation* I'm doing into my guest."

"Hmm well, you ignored me last time when I told you to stop investigating, and then you went and solved a murder!" said Sam. "Boy, did I feel like a jerk afterward."

"But you were right!" Roxy said. "It was just by chance that I solved it. It was a lucky break. But this time, I'm really out of my depth. I have to keep the influencers happy or they'll post terrible things about the Funky Cat, but this person, the one who's been untruthful, is *one* of the influencers! Oh dear. And it looks like I'm going to have to say something to the media eventually. Or they're just going to keep popping up in unexpected places. Oh dear, oh dear." She was wringing her hands and looking around the room as though the answer might lie among the racks of plastic-swathed laundry or in the churning washing machines.

Sam came up behind her and put his hands on her shoulders. "There, there. You just need to calm yourself a little. And never mind those journalists. They are like cockroaches. They scuttle away when you stand up to them."

The pressure from Sam's hands calmed Roxy, and she took a couple of deep breaths. "*Exactly* like cockroaches."

"You could just give a generic statement that yes, this thing happened. It's a terrible tragedy, that your thoughts are with the family, and you're looking forward to the case being resolved."

Roxy gulped and looked down at her lap. "That sounds like a press conference. Lots of journalists."

"It doesn't have to be like that," he said. "You can do it with one news crew. I guarantee all the other stations will pick it up."

The very thought of Roxy's face being beamed across the country, even the state—heck, the city, was terrifying.

Sam moved in front of her, and when she looked up from watching her fingers, which she was interlacing in different patterns in her lap, she saw him looking at her intently. The concern in his eyes caught her off guard.

"Just do it if you want to," he said. "If you don't, that's fine too. Just don't let fear get in the way of what you want to do."

Roxy smiled a little. "Easier said than done, though, right?"

He nodded. "Generally, yes, but don't feed fear with time, that's what I always say. It's like ripping off a band-aid —it's best just to go for it."

"And what about Johnson? And the untruthful influencer?"

"Well, that's up to you too. Do what you think would be the best for Dash."

CHAPTER THIRTY

FOR DINNER THAT evening, Nat had prepared shrimp étouffée and salmon cakes with rice and a Creole remoulade. None of the guests felt in the mood for a large, dress-up dinner, so everyone came down in their jeans and sweaters. The evening had turned cool. Lily Vashchenko even wore bright pink fluffy slippers with rabbit ears—and two-inch heels. Only Ada dressed up. She wore jeans but with towering stilettos and an emerald-green silk shirt.

Everyone—even Kathy—made a concerted attempt to talk about everything *except* Dash's death. They talked about the weather (changeable), what was planned for next year's Mardi Gras (nothing that they knew of, but they were sure it would be fun), the color of the dining room wallpaper (powder blue with shimmering beige stripes), whether all bottled water was collected from natural springs (!), and Derek's future career plans (none specific at present).

Roxy made a special effort to smile a lot at Sylvia and

engage with everything she said like she was her special friend. A raised eyebrow from Nat let her know she was overdoing it a little, so she toned it down.

Roxy was *desperate* to tell Nat what she'd found out about Sylvia, but they hadn't been alone all evening. She had to be patient. The guests would shortly be retiring for the night, and Roxy would be able to launch straight into all that she'd learned as soon as she and Nat were alone in the kitchen.

"Let me help you load the dishwasher," she heard Kathy say, as the others left for their rooms. Roxy inwardly groaned.

"But you're a guest!" Roxy protested. "I can't let you do that. Please, please, sit down in the lounge and help yourself to a drink."

"But I *insist,*" said Kathy. "I'm doing an online course in personal development, and for a challenge, we have to go out of our way to do one good deed a day." She held her head up proudly and said, "It's always good to learn and grow."

"Yes, but . . ." Nat looked a little bewildered. "Are you sure?"

"Yes," Kathy said emphatically.

Nat shook her head. "Well, okay . . . if that's really what you want."

Kathy sang Country and Western songs as she loaded the dishwasher and Nat and Roxy cleared the dining room. They waited to see if Kathy had an ulterior motive for offering to help, but when she was done, she simply gave them a huge smile and said, "Deed done for the day."

Roxy smiled back. "Thank you, Kathy. Now *please,* go ahead, and sit yourself down with a nice drink."

"Raise a glass to Dash for us," Nat added.

"I sure will," Kathy replied.

Nat closed the kitchen door behind Dash's mother as she left and waited a few moments. She whispered, "I'm not sure about her."

"She is a bit strange. Anyway, forget that. Listen to this." Roxy explained all about Sylvia being Helen and everything she'd learned.

"No way!" Nat hissed. "I *thought* there was something fishy about her."

Roxy laughed. "You think everyone's fishy, Nat."

"But even if she does appear a bit dodgy, why would she kill Dash or hurt Michael? And wasn't she asleep by the time Michael was attacked? He stayed for a good while to chat with Sage and Dr. Jack, even after the others had gone to bed. They were talking about subatomic reality and how that related to spiritual enlightenment, or something like that. Sage told me. Of course, it's all rubbish, but that doesn't change the fact that Sylvia couldn't have attacked Michael when she was here, in bed."

"I guess you're right," Roxy said. "But, she could have snuck out. I didn't lock the door until past midnight, because Ada, Lily, and Derek stayed out late."

"Well, it's *them* we need to look at, I reckon," said Nat. "Lily wanted the Hilton contract so she could have bumped off Dash to give her a better chance of landing it, Ada could have done it in revenge for Dash humiliating her, and Derek . . . well, maybe he was jealous of his brother, so much so that he killed him."

"Come on!" said Roxy. "Derek wasn't even in the city when Dash was killed."

"Good point," Nat said. "But he could have attacked

Michael. Maybe Michael's attacker wasn't the same person who killed Dash. Maybe Derek believes Michael was the murderer and was doling out his own form of justice."

"Oh, I don't know what to think," Roxy admitted. "It's just too complicated, but I can't stop thinking about it. I need to do *something*. Oh, and I found all this out because of a note someone posted under my door this afternoon. Don't you think that's strange?"

Nat stared at her. "That is weird. Who would do that? Do you recognize the handwriting?"

"Nope," said Roxy. "They wrote it all in capitals. The writing's very shaky like someone used their opposite hand."

Nat sighed. "A poison pen letter! Look, I sound so, so, *so* incredibly boring and square, I know, but you should really hand that over to Detective Johnson."

Roxy wrinkled her nose. "Yes, you're right. But, oh, you know he's going to grill me like a cheese sandwich. I'll have to psych myself up for another interview. Which reminds me, Sam still thinks I should speak to the reporters, give them a simple statement to get them off my back. One of them accosted me in the street earlier."

Nat shrugged. "Sounds like a good idea to me. Can't hurt, can it?"

"Oh, easy for you to say!" Roxy said, feeling a wave of anxiety immediately rise up and wash over her. "I'm the one who has to stand in front of all these cameras that are beaming my face across the world and say stuff that makes some kind of sense. It's terrifying."

Nat flashed her a wicked grin. "You're the boss. That means you get all the headaches, responsibility, and horrible jobs. Congratulations!" She threw her hands up in the air and laughed. "Sorry, girl. Look, I believe in you. Go ahead and do it. In fact, do it right now. Go out there and find a reporter. The more you wait around, the more afraid you'll become."

Roxy could hear her heart thumping, even in her temples! But she knew Nat was right. It was crunch time.

CHAPTER THIRTY-ONE

ROXY DID EXACTLY what Nat suggested, and trying not to think any more about what she was doing, she marched outside. She stood in the middle of the narrow cobblestoned street on which the Funky Cat Inn was located and looked up and down, straining to catch a glimpse of the woman with a mass of wavy dark hair, a flash of red lipstick, and a massive, menacing microphone. It was late in the evening. Roxy half-hoped that Mariah Morales had gone home.

"Roxy," a voice said behind her, so close that it made her flinch. She spun around and there—as if Roxy had, by thinking about her, manifested her out of thin air—was Mariah Morales, her bright red mouth stretched into a broad smile.

"Hello," Roxy said. Her voice sounded shaky and weak. Her shoulders drooped. Roxy hated that she sounded so pathetic. She instantly threw her shoulders back, lifted her chin and cleared her throat. "Hello, Ms. Morales. I want to make a statement."

"Wonderful!" Mariah said, throwing one hand up in the

air and snapping her fingers. "Sheldon, we're ready. We'll record it and send it right over to the station." She looked around the street warily. "Wouldn't want to wait for a live slot and let anyone else get their claws on *this* story." Her voice became more intense. "Sheldon, come *on!* Are you ready yet?"

"Ready," grunted Sheldon from behind her. He held the camera at chest height and the recording light came on.

Instantly Mariah slapped on her trademark smile. "And with me now is Roxy Reinhardt, manager of the Funky Cat Inn where just a few days ago famous Instagram influencer, Dashiell Davies was brutally murdered."

Mariah continued to set up the segment as Roxy heard blood thunder in her ears. She barely registered what Mariah was saying until . . .

"What would you like to say to the world about this tragedy, Ms. Reinhardt?"

Roxy's mind went blank. She couldn't get her thoughts straight. In fact, she couldn't think at all. The only thing she could do was open her mouth, let the words come, and hope she sounded somewhat lucid. She couldn't even process what she was saying, not really. All she remembered afterward was "terrible tragedy" and "Detective Johnson," "justice," and "no evidence that our hotel food was responsible." "Thank you," Roxy said at the end of her statement. She walked away, leaving Mariah to close the segment in front of Sheldon.

As she made her way back inside the Funky Cat, Roxy felt something she had never experienced in her entire life. An incredible rush of relief and pride pulsated through her like she'd been "plugged in" for the first time ever. The mint green of Elijah's Bakery in front of her, the pink façade of the Funky Cat across from it, the dark blue of the sky above, and the bright orange of the streetlights were all so intense that she felt like someone had turned up the saturation on her vision. She wanted to skip, to run, to shout, she was so pleased with herself.

She had too much energy to go back to the hotel. Instead, she decided to track down Sage. It was late, but Roxy wanted a card reading even if she still wasn't *quite* convinced she believed in them. She thought back to the reading Sage had given Sylvia. Her memory was fuzzy, but hadn't Sage said that Sylvia's story had not yet been fully released, that something about it was still unresolved?

Roxy climbed the steps to the street where Sage had her apartment, but there was no answer when she rang the bell. Roxy put her ear to the door, but she couldn't hear a gong, drumming, voices, meditation music, or any familiar noise that would indicate Sage was home. Similarly, Roxy couldn't smell the aroma of incense unfurling under the front door. She concluded that Sage wasn't in. Roxy decided to try Dr. Jack's botanica, instead. Despite the lateness of the hour, it would be open. You know, for the witches.

Roxy hurried to the magical supplies store, and stepped inside, savoring the wonderful familiar smell. She could never quite put her finger on what it was, but it was musky and sweet with notes of wood and herbs. It was like walking into a hug that you weren't quite sure you wanted.

There was no one at the cashier desk, so Roxy weaved her way through the aisles of candles, cauldrons, handcrafts, statues, soaps, and skulls. Finally, she found Dr. Jack counting essential oils on a shelf, his back to her. Before she spoke out or identified herself, he said, "Hello, Roxy. How nice to see you."

Roxy felt shivers go up her spine. "How did you know it was me?"

"You have a very distinctive aura," he said. "Especially tonight. A very particular kind of energy, expansive. Did you achieve a goal of some kind?"

Roxy was dumbstruck. "Well, I did finally talk to a reporter outside the Funky Cat, something I was very nervous about."

"Aha!" Dr. Jack said. "Well done. Now, what can I help you with?"

"I'm looking for Sage," she said.

"She was due here earlier," he replied, "but had to cancel. She's staying the night at a hotel near her client's offices. She has a very early presentation there tomorrow morning."

"Oh," Roxy said, disappointed. "I was looking for a reading."

Jack held out his arms. "Hello?" he said.

Roxy laughed. "Oh, I know, but . . ."

"No charge," he said. "Come on, I *insist*. You look like you need a good reading. Let's do a fast one. One card. Pick it." He whipped out a tarot deck from his pocket and pointed it in her direction. "Go! No thinking, now. Thinking will overwhelm your intuition."

Roxy shut her eyes and picked a card at random. It was a card with a young man holding a medallion. The medallion had a star on it. "*The Page of Pentacles,*" she read.

"A wonderful card," Dr. Jack said. He peered at her. "It means you're ready to manifest your dreams. This is a good time to start new projects. Look to the possibilities and potential of what you're doing and make concrete plans. Don't just *react* to how events unfold. Be proactive. Make things happen, Roxy. Push ahead."

CHAPTER THIRTY-TWO

ROXY WAS TRYING desperately hard to heed Detective Johnson's advice. She bustled around her room going through her early morning wakeup routine, ruminating as she did so. She was *not* going to go investigating and poking her nose in where it was not wanted. Instead, she was going to focus on making sure that her guests had the best time with her that they possibly could, given the grisly events that had occurred and the possibility that one of them was the murderer.

She decided to organize another trip for them, and an idea popped into her head while she was in the shower. This time, why not go to Marie Laveau's grave? Since the steamer captain had told her about it, it had piqued Roxy's curiosity. She'd see for herself what it was all about, and she would take her guests with her.

Roxy was undecided about what she thought of New Orleans Voodoo, but she *did* want to know about the heritage of the city. It was undoubtedly a special place. There was something in the air, a certain type of magic, and she wanted to understand what it was. It wasn't just the Cajun and Creole spices, it wasn't just the allure of Mardi Gras or the soft warmth of soulful jazz. There was a *je ne sais quoi* of the place, a sense of mystery about which Roxy didn't tire of learning.

The cemetery would undoubtedly generate interesting content for the Instagrammers, and she put her idea to the influencers over breakfast. Everyone was keen to go along. Even Ada said she would join them if only for the historical aspect of the outing. "I do not believe in such witchcraft, though," she said. "I want that noted by everyone."

"And you think I do?" Nat said pausing as she topped up the coffee pots. "It's just something you have to know about, being in New Orleans. It's not like you're going to become a Voodoo priestess tomorrow!"

Ada opened her eyes wide. There was silence at the table.

"How dare you be so impertinent!" Ada said.

"Sorry," said Nat quickly. "I didn't mean anything by it, Ada. I was joking around, that's all."

Ada continued to look outraged before looking at Lily, Sylvia, Kathy, and Derek. They were staring at her, their utensils paused in midair as they waited for this latest drama to unfold. Ada caught sight of Kathy, whose eyes were wide, her mouth forming a small "O".

It was at just that moment that Elijah arrived. Without knocking, he breezed through the front door, sashaying his way through the lounge and dining area, one hand aloft supporting three boxes of pastries piled on top of one another. "Morning, everyone!" he cried without stopping. He turned to push the kitchen door with his behind. He gave Derek a little wave and a grin before disappearing into the kitchen.

Elijah's appearance had pierced the heavy atmosphere

and Ada relaxed. She gave Nat a small smile. "That's okay, I forgive you. But don't do it again," she finished softly. Roxy breathed a sigh of relief, and Nat hurried into the kitchen, glad to have a bolthole.

"Let's go to Marie Laveau's this morning and get a light lunch afterward," Roxy said brightly, keen to dispel any lingering remnants of tension. "Because I don't know about you, but I'm not keen on going at night."

Everyone felt the same. So she, Nat, Lily, Sylvia, Ada, Kathy, and Derek set off toward the old cemetery soon after breakfast. Roxy also called Evangeline to see if she wanted to join them, but she said, "I've been one hundred times before, cher, since I was a little girl. My mama had plenty a wish granted by the Voodoo Queen. Say hello to her for me, won't you?"

Michael didn't want to come either. "It's just a tourist trap, Roxy. I want to experience the *real* spiritual heritage of New Orleans. Plus, my head still aches."

Roxy thought his response a little rude but didn't say anything. She kept what he'd been through at the forefront of her mind. She brushed off his dismissal and prepared herself to act as tour guide.

Roxy had thought that visiting the spot in the morning would take away the eeriness of the place, but she was wrong. The Saint Louis cemetery was incredibly quiet, the silence spooky. They could hear every footstep as they walked deeper and deeper into the cemetery. It was like walking through a miniature, abandoned city. Eventually, they came upon Marie Laveau's grave. It was a huge gray box of a mausoleum nestled in among those of others. X signs were scrawled all over the tomb, some with rings around them.

"This feels too weird," whispered Lily, shivering even though the sun was out.

Roxy felt the same. It seemed as though even the birds had stopped singing. She told herself not to be so ridiculous, that Marie Laveau was long dead (1881!), and any stories of her spirit lingering were just superstition.

"Marie Laveau was a hairdresser by day," Roxy told the assembled group, "but at night she was known as the Voodoo Queen, sought after for her potions and charms. She was immensely powerful and many people were enthralled by her. It is said that even politicians, lawyers, businessmen, and the wealthy were influenced by her."

Ada hovered at the back of the group with a guidebook. "This is very interesting from a *historical* perspective," she said. Her voice shook a little.

Just then, they heard a voice coming from behind the mausoleum. "You come to see me?" the voice bellowed, in thick, foreboding tones. Everyone jumped. Ada screamed. Lily launched herself across the group and grabbed Roxy's arm.

Derek jumped out from behind the grave. "Haha!" he cried, showing more energy in this one moment than he had in the entire time he'd been in their company. "I scared you all, didn't I? The looks on your faces! I should have recorded it on my phone! Now *that's* an Instagram story!"

"Derek!" Kathy scolded him. "You nearly gave us all a heart attack!"

"Who was the one who screamed?" Derek asked, a sneer playing on his lips. Ada stared at him in stony silence.

"It was Ada," Lily said, seriously. "But I don't blame her. That was really scary. Perhaps you should do tours around here. You would be great at scaring the tourists half to death. Some people like that kind of thing."

"That's an idea," Derek said. He dug Lily in the ribs with his elbow. She frowned and moved away from him.

Roxy was absolutely furious. He was sabotaging her outing, turning it into a highly unpleasant experience. How could he be so mean? "Does anyone want to make a wish?" she asked to distract them from Derek's prank. "When you make your wish you have to turn around, shout it out, and mark your "X" on the tomb. When it comes true the custom is to return here, circle your "X," and leave a gift. That's why there's all these flowers and beads. Is anyone going to make a wish?"

"I don't know if I dare," said Sylvia.

"Oh, I will!" said Kathy. "I will ask for justice for my son."

Kathy walked up to the tomb, turned around and shouted out, "Justice for my son's murder! Dashiell Davies!" She took a pen from her bag and marked an X on the grave. "The Voodoo Queen better help me," she muttered. "I hope she and Jesus work together!"

"I wouldn't say that if I were you," said Ada.

CHAPTER THIRTY-THREE

KATHY TURNED TO Ada, her eyes devoid of any life. She didn't even smile, not even a forced one. "Don't tell me what I should and shouldn't do," she said. "When your child has been murdered, then and only then will you be qualified to give *me* advice."

"Sorry," Ada had the decency to mutter.

Roxy took that as a cue to leave the cemetery and took them to an Italian restaurant for lunch. Pasta and pizza was always a comforting choice, and it felt like they all needed some solace. The restaurant she took them to—Mandinelli's —was famous for suffusing traditional Italian food with Creole and Cajun spice to make a truly unique New Orleans foodie experience.

As they settled down to eat, Roxy checked her phone. There was a message for her on the Funky Cat Instagram profile. A private message. She clicked on it. She guessed it was to discuss a booking. But it wasn't.

Check this out.

Attached was a video. Looking furtively around to see if any of the group was watching, Roxy pressed "play." All she saw was a jerky video of a pair of men's booted feet. But then she heard the audio.

"Do you see how you're talking to me?" Roxy thought it might have been Dash's voice, but she wasn't sure. *"I'm recording you!"* The voices were quiet, so Roxy brought the phone up to her ear. She kept switching between listening and looking at the screen.

"Stop that!" This time it was a different voice. The camera jerked upward, and there was Michael, glaring into it. She was sure the other voice was Dash's now. Michael called Dash a name and slapped the camera out of his hand so that the view from the device jerked and twisted. It ended up facing a ceiling.

"No way," Roxy whispered to herself. Maybe Kathy had been right about Michael after all. Maybe he wasn't so nice.

"Why are you so against the Hilton idea?" It was Dash's voice again. He sounded perplexed and angry.

Michael replied. *"Because the Hilton idea is ridiculous! You and I agreed we wouldn't go down the commercial route because . . ."*

Dash: *"No, you decided, and I have to go along with it like I always do! But I'm not doing it anymore, Michael. I'm not! I swear to you!"*

Dash was really angry now. Roxy heard Michael let out a growl of anger, and the video cut off. Roxy sat still, her heart thumping.

"Are you okay, Roxy?" Kathy said, leaning over to her.

Roxy moved the phone out of her view. "Oh yes, I'm fine," she said quickly, smiling at her.

Kathy frowned. "You don't *look* okay."

"I was . . . well, someone messaged me about a booking and asked for a discount for a certain number of nights. I was just trying to do the math in my head." She forced a laugh. "Math isn't my strong point." Neither was lying. Roxy felt, and was sure she looked, uncomfortable.

"Oh, let me take a look," said Kathy, holding her hand out for the phone. "I used to be a middle school math teacher."

"It's okay, don't worry about it," said Roxy with a smile. "I've forwarded it to my work email already. It'll be fine. Now I just need to head to the bathroom real quick. Please excuse me."

Roxy dashed to the restroom at the back of the restaurant. She wanted a minute alone with the phone to reply to the direct message. But she couldn't. There was no bar for her to type her reply into. She looked at the profile of the account that had sent her the video. It was clearly a fake. There was no profile picture and only the name 'XgXgXg' which, of course, meant nothing.

Roxy slipped the phone into her pocket and sighed. She cast a glance at herself in the mirror. She looked the same as she always did—slim, slight, and small, with a blonde pixie haircut and a face that others told her was beautiful, but which looked just ordinary to her. There was a strength, a steeliness, to Roxy's eyes though. Just then the door to the bathroom burst open. She flinched. Kathy barreled through the door.

"I have to use the little girl's room too," Kathy said. "And I thought I could help you with that math."

Roxy smiled. She was starting to feel a little irritated. "Seriously, it's all right," she said. "Have you decided what you're ordering?"

"No, it all looks too delicious to choose!" said Kathy. "I do have a favor to ask, though."

"Sure, what is it?"

"You know we've been talking about holding a celebration of Dash's life?"

"Uh-huh?"

"Well, we've decided to hold a large outdoor event on the weekend. I spoke to the city about it this morning. Since Dashiell admittedly *did* love a good time, we thought a street party would be the right thing to do. That way, we can invite his fans as well as his friends."

"I think he'd have loved that."

"So my question is, can you be one of the caterers? I know you can't do *everything*—I'll get other people to cook food too—but I've so enjoyed the cuisine at the Funky Cat that I'd love for you to get involved."

Roxy hugged her. "Of course, Kathy. We'd be honored."

They went back to the table, and Roxy played the role of carefree host with apparent ease. But inside, her mind was *tick tick tick* with ideas. Who had sent the video? It had shown her a very dark side of Michael. Maybe Dash and he weren't such great friends, after all. Maybe, just maybe, Michael had *faked* his own attack. Maybe it hadn't happened like he said at all.

CHAPTER THIRTY-FOUR

"**E**XCUSE ME!" JOHNSON said. "Attention!" He looked annoyed. "And turn off that darned radio."

"Yes?" Evangeline said, twisting toward him, her hands on her hips. "What is it?"

Unannounced, Detective Johnson had arrived at the Funky Cat on the morning of the street party to celebrate Dash's life.

He turned up at the worst possible time—when everyone was hard at work in the kitchen. Lily looked stylish and impractical in slacks, heels, and a silk blouse, but she had brought her own apron and rubber gloves. Sylvia was there in dungarees and a work shirt. Derek showed up cloaked in a hoodie. The guests had generously offered to help with the food preparations. They'd eaten breakfast at six a.m. so they could be in the kitchen by seven, and no one had made a murmur of complaint. Even the glamorous Ada, who wore a Versace tracksuit, hadn't pitched a fit when she was splashed by the crab boil.

Evangeline, of course, was the kitchen manager and

behaved in a way that was rather Gordon Ramsay-esque although without the incessant cursing. She certainly wasn't going to pamper Sylvia, Lily, and Ada just because they were Instagram stars. Roxy bit her lip at times when she heard Evangeline barking orders at them, but the truth was no one seemed to mind.

It was an all-hands situation so they rolled up their sleeves, literally in Sylvia's case, and got on with their tasks. Evangeline's old radio blasted out happy jazz tunes that had them dancing around the kitchen, and there were back slaps and shouts of laughter as they happily made cornbread patties, stirred gumbo, and assembled po' boys. Everyone seemed enthused by the prospect of a party. Derek almost raised a smile at one point. His mother, Kathy, was with Sam. They were setting up at the site of the party—hanging flags, arranging the stage, and organizing where all the caterers' tables would go while back in the Funky Cat kitchen Roxy teamed with Lily to make what seemed like a million *oysters en brochette.*

Sharing the tasks, Roxy and Lily skewered the oysters, bacon, and onion before rolling each skewer in cornflour. Later at the event, they would deep-fry them. They would also cut toast into triangles and brush them with a Meunière sauce made from parsley, lemon, brown butter, and red wine vinegar. After they had been fried, the cooked oysters, onion, and bacon would be served on top of the toast, and a twist of salt and pepper would complete the dish. Roxy had only made it once and that time under Evangeline's watchful eye, but today Evangeline had some ten other dishes going. They were on their own, but there was an easy, warm atmosphere of camaraderie in the kitchen and they were all focused on their tasks. Roxy's mind was as far away from Dash's murder or any other disaster as it could get.

That was until Detective Johnson showed up. Immediately the happy bubble around them burst with a pop. It was almost like Johnson carried a big pin with him.

"Look, I don't know what it is with this place, but any time something happens around here it seems to involve y'all. So I'm here to tell you no messing around today, y'hear? No funny business. This event is for Dashiell Davies. The police department has been liaising with his mother, and if *anything* untoward happens, the attention of your local law enforcement will shift to the Funky Cat faster than you can say 'Instagram'. Is that clear?"

Roxy peered around to see the influencers looking taken aback. Ada glared at Johnson, Lily looked as though there was a nasty smell under her nose while Sylvia, like Evangeline, stood with her hands on her hips. Derek seemed to merge with the pots and pans as he tried to make himself invisible. The guests clearly weren't used to being spoken to like that. Roxy, on the other hand, had a little more experience. She walked up to the detective and kept her voice low. "Of course, Detective," she said quietly. She hoped he would match her tone. She was mistaken.

"Good!" he bellowed even louder than before. "And don't think that because y'all are some kind of famous in the strange world you live in that I won't zero in on you. Behave, alright? The law has no respect for celebrity or anything else. Law's the law."

"Thank you, Detective Johnson," said Roxy calmly. "We'll make sure to remain law-abiding. You have my word on that."

"Don't you rush me!" he said. "It is very likely the murderer will be in the crowd today so we'll be keeping a close but discreet eye on the proceedings. Watch yourselves, okay?" Roxy heard the word "murderer" with a jolt.

Johnson continued, "The toxicology reports are back. Mr. Davies was incapacitated with a form of poison, then suffocated." Johnson proceeded to stride around the room, thumbs tucked into his belt loops that sat under his large belly. He looked at each person carefully, and the food they were preparing, before moving on. He reminded Roxy of a Wild West sheriff inspecting his usual suspects.

It got so quiet in the kitchen as he did this that every single bubble popping at the top of a boil could be heard. Roxy could hear *tap-tap-tap* as Derek gently banged his model airplane against the chrome counter. Despite the news of the manner of his brother's death, he seemed unfazed.

Eventually, Johnson warily said, "Alright." He watched Roxy out of the corner of his eye as if she were some criminal mastermind and the three influencers and Derek were her henchmen. "Well, I'll be seeing y'all later." Roxy shook her head as soon as he was out the door.

"What was *that* about?" Nat burst out when he'd gone. She shook herself like a dog. "I can't *stand* that guy!"

"Neither can I," Ada said.

Their view of Johnson was something both Nat and Ada could agree on. They looked at each other a little more warmly.

"Let's try and forget about him," Roxy said, switching the music back on. The radio station was playing a compilation of popular Nat King Cole tunes. The lively melody of *Route 66* rippled from the radio. Evangeline and Sylvia starting singing softly along, shaking their hips as they continued to prepare the food. Soon they were all moving at least one body part in time to the music. Well, not Derek, but even he didn't leave the room.

"Sing us something, Nat, cher," Evangeline said.

"Nah, I have to save my voice for later. They like the big tunes do this crowd. Besides I can't do better than ole Nat, now can I?"

"You're singing at the event?" Roxy asked.

"Yep, with Sam and Elijah. Kathy asked us."

"Ah, that's nice."

Roxy would have been perfectly happy to while away the rest of the morning making oyster skewers with Lily, listening to some mellow jazz, and forgetting about everything else. The repetitive rhythm of the cooking was cathartic, and the smells of Creole spices were soothing. But it wasn't to be. A short while later, Kathy bustled into the kitchen looking for her. She flashed a huge smile, hooked her arm into Roxy's, and pulled her out of the kitchen. "Come with me, girl." They walked out of the front door and into the cobbled street.

"Wow!" Roxy said.

CHAPTER THIRTY-FIVE

ROWS AND ROWS and rows of flags had been hung, strung from one side of the alleyway to the other, in every color Roxy could imagine. When they came out onto the main street, Roxy could see that the flags continued, tied to streetlights and storefronts and electricity poles, anything that was high enough. They continued as far as Roxy could see.

"Look," Kathy said, "they run all the way from your door to the party.

"Kathy!" Roxy said. "Dash would have *loved* this!"

Immediately, Kathy's cheerful smile turned into heartrending sobs. She collapsed onto Roxy. Being that Kathy was the bigger woman and Roxy was tiny, Roxy staggered backward under the heavier woman's weight. With some effort, she managed to right herself, but Kathy crumpled down onto the sidewalk. She stayed there and curled up in a ball, her head on her knees. She began to cry and cry and cry. She just didn't stop.

At first, Roxy patted her on the shoulder, and said, "Kathy, Kathy," but her voice was drowned out by the woman's cries. Eventually, Roxy sat next to her, her arm around her shoulder and her heart hurting as she listened to Kathy's sobs, unable to do or say anything to help.

They stayed sitting on the curb for what seemed like an age. Vehicles passed by, their drivers and passengers staring at them, and Roxy was *so* glad not to see Mariah Morales and her ilk prowling around with their cameras, ready to capture the scene and splash it across the state news. There was no sign of any reporters at all.

As Roxy continued to comfort Kathy, she spotted the priest who had performed Dash's memorial service as he came around the corner. He walked toward them.

"Father Daniel!" Roxy called out. Kathy looked up.

The priest picked up his pace when he recognized them and with gentle hands brought Kathy to her feet. He wiped her tears away with his soft, fat fingers. "May the Lord bring you peace, my child."

Kathy blubbed, "I . . . don't . . . think . . . that's . . . possible, Father!"

"It will be, with time," he said. "Put your trust in the Lord. *Choose* to put your trust in the Lord."

"Okay," Kathy said like an obedient little girl. "I can do that . . . I think. Thank you."

"You will be blessed for your faith," he said. "There, there . . ." Kathy visibly calmed at his words and began to breathe normally.

Father John turned to Roxy. "I came here to see you."

Roxy was a little taken aback. "Yes, Father?"

"I was wondering if you would speak at the event today. Of course, Kathy is speaking. Derek is not, due to his shy nature. Michael is paying a tribute to Dashiell, their work and fans. We, Kathy and I, that is, talked earlier, and wondered if you would like to say something. As a sort of representative of the city of New Orleans."

Roxy bit her lip. "Me? But I'm not even *from* here."

"Yes," he said. "I can tell that by your accent. But you're a businesswoman here now, and that means you are part of our community. I have talked to Michael too. He explained that you were a kind person. Perhaps you saw some qualities in Dash that you admired and that you can speak to?"

"Oh, yes," Roxy said. "Of course. He was adventurous and wild and brave, for sure. He was very encouraging too, and certainly knew how to have a good time!"

The priest nodded triumphantly. "That's that, then. You'll give a small speech?"

Roxy's stomach lurched. Speaking in front of a huge crowd of people wasn't her idea of fun. They were expecting thousands—not only local residents but many, many fans. Many more than turned out at the funeral. This time Dash's followers had had plenty of notice, and people were traveling from all over the country. Some were even coming from Europe! Roxy looked at Kathy, hoping that she would say it was inappropriate.

But she didn't. She looked tearfully in Roxy's direction. "Please do," she said. "It would mean a lot to me."

Roxy gulped. "Okay," she said quietly. Her eyes were wary. The priest looked at her quizzically. She cleared her throat and straightened up. "Sure," said Roxy, more confidently now. "I'd love to."

"Excellent!" Kathy gave a little jump and clapped her hands. "Now, I want to show you the rest of the preparations," she said. "And to show you where you guys need to bring the food later."

The trio started to walk. Kathy went a little way ahead and Roxy strolled alongside Father John.

"Thank you for helping Kathy and Derek like this, Father. I know you've been a huge support to them," Roxy said.

"Ah, no worries, young lady. It's my job. They've been dealt a terrible hand," the priest replied.

"Do you think Kathy will be alright?"

"With the love of God and her faith, I believe in time she will be."

"And Derek?"

"That, I don't know. I don't know the young man well. I only met him at the funeral service. I don't think he shares his mother's faith. You take care of them in your way and I will do so in mine. Together we'll do the very best for them."

"That we will, Father."

CHAPTER THIRTY-SIX

"**W**OW, IT'S NEARLY ten a.m. already! We're starting in an hour," Kathy cried as she showed Roxy around the party site. "Here's where you'll speak." The stage was flanked with beautiful pillars graced with streamers and crisscrossed with more flags in bright colors. "Here's where you'll serve your food."

Roxy saw a few partygoers come down the street and glanced at her watch. "Look! People are trickling in already! I'd better get everyone to load their food into the van and bring it down. Where are all the other caterers, Kathy?"

Kathy bit her lip and looked down at her phone. "I told everyone to come at ten thirty. Hopefully, that won't be too late!"

Roxy smiled encouragingly. "I'm sure it will be absolutely fine. Come on, why don't we go back to the hotel and get ready?"

Kathy smiled. "Sure! I think we'd better go at a jog, or we'll be late for our own party!"

"Okay, let's hurry!" said Roxy.

They headed back to the hotel quickly, and Roxy went into her room. Before changing, she grabbed a pen and pad and dashed into the kitchen where only Evangeline remained. Everyone else was upstairs getting changed into their party clothes.

"Aren't you getting your glad rags on, Evangeline?" Roxy asked.

"Oh, no, cher," the older lady replied. "I'll be headin' home. Can't be doin' with all these street parties anymore. I've been jumpin' up in carnival since I could jump . . . naw, since *before* I could jump. Too many parties will take the party spirit right out of you. I can't get excited anymore. Too old."

"Yeah, I get it," said Roxy. "I'm not one for parties myself. I always *thought* I wanted to go, but when I'd get there I'd wish I was at home curled up with a good book." She was jabbering, rushing through the kitchen drawers like a hurricane.

"You just take this food and feed it to all those young people, y'hear? What you lookin' for, cher?" Evangeline asked.

"I'm looking for some bags."

Evangeline pulled open a drawer. She dragged out a small pile of brown paper bags and held them out. The elderly woman looked at Roxy quizzically. "What do you want 'em for?"

"I'm just giving everyone a little goodie bag," Roxy said. "You know, seeing as it's nearly their time to leave us."

"Great idea," said Evangeline. "What are you puttin' in 'em?"

Roxy paused, her eyes resting on bottles of spices lined up on the window ledge. "Cooking spices!" she said, hurrying over. "I-I-I'm gonna give each one of them a jar of your special Cajun spice blend, so they can make their own New Orleans-style meals when they get home."

Evangeline sniffed. "It's not a matter of having the right spices. N'awlins cookin' is much deeper than that. There's soul involved."

"Oh, I know, you're right," said Roxy. "But at least they can try. And it's a nice gesture."

Evangeline nodded. "Hmph, awright, but I hope you're not expectin' me to help you bag it all up, cher. I'm still stuffin' these tartlets."

"Oh, but I need your help. I don't know the recipe."

"I don't make it up each time I use it, you know."

"You don't?"

"Nah, I make up a batch every so often." She pointed to the walk-in pantry in the corner. "Top shelf, back left corner.

Roxy dashed over to the pantry and seeing a huge mason jar full of spice blend on the highest shelf, climbed onto a step stool to retrieve it.

Evangeline peered over her tartlets as Roxy staggered out of the pantry carrying the glass jar that was nearly as big as she was and just as heavy. "Do you need a hand with that?"

"No, it's fine!" said Roxy, breathlessly. "I got this." She strained to place the jar carefully down on the counter and took a breath before saying, "Oh! I need containers."

"Don't you worry, cher, I got some lovely glass jars, just the right size. I was savin' them for my tomato basil jelly, but you can use 'em and I'll get some more." Evangeline pointed to the pantry again. "Box on the floor on the left, just as you go in the door."

"You're a lifesaver, Evangeline."

Evangeline smiled fondly as she watched Roxy dash

back into the pantry and come out again carrying a card-board box full of unused canning jars. Roxy spooned the spice mix into six jars.

"I've got some labels somewhere here." Evangeline rooted around in a drawer and brought out some brown tags. "Now, you have lovely handwritin'. Write *Evangeline's Cajun Spice Mix* on 'em and tie them around the rim before you put the lid on."

Roxy did as she was told. As she wrote, she asked, "Tell me, what's in your mix, Evangeline? What makes it so fantastic?"

"Well, there's the usual paprika, garlic powder, cayenne pepper, oregano, onion powder, thyme, salt, and pepper."

"And?" Roxy pressed. "Isn't there something special you put in it? Something your grandmomma passed down to you?"

"Ah, they would be my special ingredients."

"And what are they?"

"Well, that would be tellin', wouldn't it?"

Roxy looked at her. "But won't you ever tell me? What will I do when this batch runs out?" She waved over to the huge jar that she estimated contained enough spices to last at least five years. "I won't be able to replicate your meals if you don't tell. Our guests will be disappointed if I don't use it in the cooking."

Evangeline looked at Roxy's sweet, innocent, slightly bewildered face. "Guess you're right. I did invite you to run this place after all."

"So what are they?"

CHAPTER THIRTY-SEVEN

E VANGELINE LEANED OVER to whisper in Roxy's ear. "Lemongrass and a touch of saffron."

Roxy frowned. "But, but . . . aren't they mostly used in Indian and Asian cuisines?"

Evangeline tapped her nose. "Exactly, cher."

Roxy paused, then smiled, nodding. "Okay, okay. Unconventional, I'll give you that, but okay."

After she'd attached the labels, Roxy wrapped ribbon around the necks of the jars, finishing them with a bow. She tightened the lids on the jars and they were ready.

Roxy counted out the brown bags and labeled them, one each for Lily, Ada, Kathy, Derek, Sylvia, and Michael. Writing Michael's name made her think of the speech she was due to give later but even that couldn't distract her at that moment. She slipped a jar of spices into each bag and a note she had written into one of them.

Roxy heard footsteps come down the grand stairway outside the kitchen. She folded over the tops of the bags, popped them all onto a tray and rushed into the hallway. She stood in front of the door determined that not a single one of her guests would leave before she'd handed them their bags. She'd track Michael down at the event.

Nat, Kathy, Derek, Ada, Lily, and Sylvia gathered in the hallway. They looked great in their bright colors. Well, in all honesty, Derek didn't look *that* great but then he never did. His eyes were dull and sunken, and he looked moody. As ever, he was fidgeting with his model airplane. Roxy felt herself feeling a little sorry for him.

"Come on, let's go," Nat said. She made for the front door.

Roxy dashed forward and put herself between Nat and the assembled group.

"Hi, everyone," she said brightly.

Nat, who was in black as usual but wore her turquoise sparkly Doc Martens and a matching neckerchief, said, "Is Sam here yet?" She peered out of the door. "He's going to have to drive all the way inside the alleyway. There's no *way* we can lug all the food up to the street."

"Nope, he's not here yet," said Roxy, still facing the group.

"I'll call him," Nat said, pulling out her phone. Then she nodded at the brown bags. "What are those?"

"Oh yes," Roxy said as if she'd forgotten them. The tray they lay on might as well have been burning hot for all she was able to ignore it. She addressed the group. "They're just a little thank-you from those of us at the Funky Cat. For staying with us. Something to remind you of New Orleans when you get home. Make sure to open them in private, though. I've included something pers—Oh!" The front door to the Funky Cat opened suddenly, pitching Roxy forward and sending the brown bags on her tray flying to the floor.

"I'm so sorry, Roxy!" Sage said as she walked in. "Are you alright?"

Roxy was fine, but at that moment she wasn't concerned about herself. Lily had reached down and was picking up the bags. She was handing them out indiscriminately!

"No, wait . . ." Roxy looked on in horror. But it was too late.

"Thank you so much, Roxy," Sylvia was saying.

"Yes, thank you, Roxy. You're too kind," Kathy said.

"I think I'd better put this in my room. It'll get lost at the street party," Ada added.

As everyone headed to their respective rooms to deposit their gifts, Roxy was left in the hallway holding one bag— Michael's. Nat looked at her perplexed. "What was all that about?"

Roxy shook her head. "Nothing, absolutely nothing."

Nat shrugged. "Oh, come on! Don't be a spoilsport. We still have to load all the food into Sam's van, and he's not even here yet."

Roxy fixed Nat with a glare. "Nothing is going on, all right?" she said. "Come on, let's sort out the food."

They went into the kitchen and began stacking the dishes on a rolling cart. "By the way," Nat said, avoiding eye contact with Roxy. "I just want to say that if ever I come across as a bit of a jerk, I'm very sorry. I know I get a bit edgy and a little inappropriate at times, and I also know that's no excuse. I get anxious, you see. It makes me a bit mad. Sorry, Rox."

"It's alright," said Roxy, finding a smile from some-where. "I understand. Just be careful. Take deep breaths, that's what I do. And if you see me blink rapidly five times in a row, you'll know what it means, okay?"

"Yes! It can be our secret code!" Nat said with a smile.

"That'll do!" Roxy said, laughing. She gave Nat a quick side hug. "You know I love you, Nat."

"I love you too, Rox. Thank you for keeping me on here." Nat's eyes shone.

"Come on, none of that. We've got work to do. Let's hurry up with this lot."

"I'll go and enlist some help," Nat said. She left the kitchen, soon returning accompanied by Lily and Ada. Sam came in behind them.

"Hi, Roxy," Sam said, his deep, gravelly voice as seductive as ever.

"Hi, Sam," she said, briskly. She had no time for flirting, not today. "Thanks for coming to help."

They transported dish after dish of food out to Sam's van while making sure to save some space for Elijah, who carried over piles of boxes of pastries from the bakery. When Roxy picked up the last set of plates, she turned to Evangeline, who was now loading the dishwasher. "Thank you, Evangeline, for helping us! What would we do without you?"

Evangeline came over, drying her hands on a towel. She put her arm around Roxy's shoulder. "I know what you're up to," she said quietly.

Roxy's eyes widened. "You do?"

Evangeline grimaced but pulled Roxy to her. "I recognize a fellow warrior when I see one. You do your best and seek justice. I know you need to do that for that young man. It's just in your nature like it is in mine. But be careful. Promise me that, okay? You're out in a big crowd. Small things have the tendency to get dangerous in crowds. Even carnival can get crazy. Just promise old Evangeline that you'll be careful."

"I promise," said Roxy, relaxing. For once, she didn't feel nervous or anxious, even with such an abundance of warnings. "I'll be fine. Don't worry about me. Like you said, I just want to see justice done."

Evangeline gave her an affectionate smile. "You know, cher, you're more like me than I thought. The first day you came in here you was like a timid little mouse. Like your cat coulda eaten you whole." She laughed. "Sorry, cher. But now, you're somethin' pretty different. The moxie's strong in you. Moxie Roxy." She laughed and patted her on the shoulder. "Run along, sugar. I know you'll do great."

"Thanks, Evangeline!"

Roxy rushed out and packed the last of the food into the van. Sage, Nat, and Elijah had already led the influencers, Kathy, and Derek out of the alleyway—they were walking to the party. They couldn't get lost because the street decorations guiding their way. Roxy planned to walk with them, but since they had already left, she swung herself into the van's passenger seat beside Sam.

"Hey, pretty lady," he said, giving her the half-smile that made her kneecaps feel like they were melting.

"Hey," Roxy replied softly.

CHAPTER THIRTY-EIGHT

"IT LOOKS AMAZING," Roxy said.

The block over by the river where the party was being held was normally a rundown industrial area. Now it was alive with color.

"Kathy sure doesn't play around, does she?" Sam said, sliding into a parking space.

Roxy spoke sadly. "I guess for your murdered son, you'd do anything. Money, effort, time, no object."

"Indeed," said Sam. "She must also be very determined. She would have needed a permit. How did she get around Detective Johnson to pull this off? Did he find a compassionate side?"

Roxy looked at him. "Compassionate? Him? He came to speak to us all this morning. He stared us down, each and every one of us, like we had murdered Dash in cold blood." The truth was, one of them *had* murdered Dash in cold blood.

Once Sam had parked, Roxy slid out of her seat and got to unloading. Lots of people were arriving now, all wearing bright colors, laughing and joking and drinking. One vendor had started up a bar at the side of the street. A crew was setting up a modern sound system on the stage while a wall of enormous speakers stood to one side. It looked like the event was going to be *loud*.

Roxy smiled at the scene, her feelings bittersweet. Dash had so wanted to experience the joy of New Orleans for himself, but he hadn't had the chance. Roxy hadn't known him well or for long, but she knew that he loved to grab life by the horns, to explore, to learn, to grow, and above all to *experience*. Roxy doubted he'd *ever* have settled down in one place like his mother wanted him to. He was an adventurer, right down to his bones. Excitement coursed through his veins. Wind was in his sails. There was always something to be enthusiastic about, some new territory to conquer. Now that was all over.

But Roxy looked over the growing crowd and felt something move deep within her. People were here celebrating. They clearly loved Dash's message. It touched the hearts of strangers, of people everywhere. And they had been so affected that they had made long journeys to be at the party today, to celebrate Dash one last time.

Roxy hoped that she would be able to absorb his message into her life too. In fact, it felt like she had done so a little already. Where she had allowed her anxieties and fears to clip her wings, she now felt herself growing more expansive. Where she had seen problems, she now saw possibilities. Where she had seen danger, she saw adventure. She also recognized that she had the potential to be a leader.

She knew it wasn't just Dash who had helped her. It was a sprinkle of Sage who gave Roxy the confidence that everything would be all right. It was a touch of Evangeline, who was so no-nonsense that Roxy now saw many of her anxieties as simply plain silly. It was a dusting of Elijah, who just like the sugar he scattered over his pastries, showed her how to have fun. It was a smidgeon of Sam, who always encouraged her to "go for it". And it was a nip of Nat, whose "Nat-itude" and big heart pulled no punches.

Roxy realized how far she had come since she'd climbed onto the bus headed for New Orleans a few months before. She smiled to herself as she methodically unloaded Sam's van and placed all the food on their table. There were a *lot* of dishes, and it took a good while, especially as Nat, Kathy, Derek, and the influencers were nowhere to be seen.

Roxy saw that Michael was there, sitting behind the podium on the stage. He was staring into space. She walked over and handed him his bag with the jar of spices, gave him a sympathetic nod, but otherwise left him alone. She saw him briefly look inside the bag before looking up again to resume staring at the horizon.

Before long, old school reggae began to play. It *totally* lifted the vibe, and both Roxy and Sam couldn't help briefly doing a little dance. Roxy imagined herself being so bold as to rock right up to him and dance *together* but she tamped her thought down. She couldn't afford to be distracted.

"I wonder where Nat and the others are. I haven't seen them, have you?" she said to him.

"No," said Sam. "But if I know Nat, she'll be at one of the cookout grills."

"*That's* true," said Roxy. Nat loved her grilled chicken, but Roxy was starting to get worried. Where were the others?

The crowd had really grown now. It was getting more

and more difficult to pick anyone out of it. Roxy made her way up onto the podium, and peered around, looking for Nat. Thank goodness she loved to wear black, at least. For once she would stand out among this sea of color!

Finally, Roxy *did* see her and the rest of the group. And, sure enough, they were standing by a barbecue. It was on the other side of the crowd. "We've got all the food in the world here!" Roxy said to Nat when she sauntered over. "Yet you run off to the first man with a pair of tongs!"

"I worked in that kitchen this morning until I was sweating like a crawfish," said Nat. "Heck, probably *smelling* like a crawfish. I needed something different for my palate." She ripped some meat off the chicken leg she held, looking around at the party, the colors of the crowd, the music, the food, and the way people were dancing. It was starting to look like a music festival. She saw Sage and Elijah dancing, Sage's slow and lazy moves contrasting with Elijah's peppier, upbeat ones that picked up the staccato off-beats of the reggae rhythm. "This is pretty amazing."

"Are you ready for your speech?" Sam called over.

"My what?" Roxy asked.

"Your speech, aren't you saying something? Kathy said she was going to ask you."

"Yeah, she did." The truth was that Roxy had forgotten all about making a speech. Now that things were really rocking, though, she was starting to feel edgy.

Kathy didn't look too great, either. She had on her trade-mark smile and a full face of makeup, but her skin under-neath was pale, and her blusher stood out too brightly on her cheeks. Her blue eye shadow looked wrong too, like she had made herself up as a clown. Her hands shook.

As the influencers helped themselves to food, Roxy

sidled up to Dash's mom. She slipped her hand in that of the older woman. "It's going to be okay, I promise." Kathy looked like she was about to vomit.

Before long, Father John stood up on the podium and addressed the crowd. "Hello, New Orleans!" he boomed.

CHAPTER THIRTY-NINE

"GREETINGS TO YOU all," Father John said into the microphone, more quietly this time. "We are gathered here to celebrate the life of Dashiell Davies in the vivid style that he was known for. His associate, Michael O'Sullivan, has put together a video montage of Dash's life. Please enjoy this tribute."

The priest stepped aside, and the crowd quieted to watch the huge screen. Roxy turned and craned her neck to see.

What followed was a beautiful montage of pictures and videos: of Dash on top of a mountain, of Dash skydiving, of Dash fooling around at some Hawaiian resort doing the hula on the beach under the twinkling stars, of Dash hanging out of a train in India, of Dash waving underwater while scuba diving. *Man,* this guy had done so much.

And how he laughed as he did it all! How he smiled! He had so much light in him, and it beamed across the crowd. People began to cry, and Roxy found a tear slipping down her own cheek.

Then Michael's voice thundered out from the speakers, a recording over the video.

"Dash, you were a hero—my hero—one of the world's brave people, one who refused to compromise, one who refused to play the game, and one who refused to stop dreaming. You lived life to the full in every moment, in every sense. You never said no. You always said yes. You never said, 'It's not possible.' You always said, 'How can we make this happen?' My life is forever changed because of you, and so too are the lives of millions of others. I know you wanted the world to relax because you told me that so many times.

"You know what, buddy? I regret a lot of things. I regret the way I spoke to you sometimes. I regret that I ever told you to be serious, or be realistic, or to take your time. Especially that last one, because there *was* no time to waste. And you knew it. You just went at life, full speed. You DASHED! Your name suited you down to the ground.

"You wanted to build schools, dig wells, build solar power and clean water systems, give people jobs, the tools to support themselves and their families. When we had money, you gave it all away." Over the sound of the tribute, a yell rose from the middle of the crowd. The crowd shushed and Michael's voice carried on speaking without interruption. "I swear, buddy, you didn't get the chance to do everything you dreamed of, but I'll do it, and I'll do it for you. I've been close to the edge, but I have a reason to live now—your memory, your mission, and your spirit live on in me. I'll do it, buddy. And I know you'll be watching me do it from the other side."

Now people were crying in earnest. Even though it was daylight, they had turned on their phone's flashlights and were waving them above their heads. Father John called Kathy up to the stage.

Kathy had rubbed her eyes so much that she had black rings around them where her eye makeup had smudged. All her vitality and her brave, cheerful smile had gone. She was a broken woman.

She went up to the mic and began to speak. Her voice choked with tears. "I was going to come up here and say so many good things about Dashiell. But I can't." She dropped her chin onto her chest, and it stayed there. Roxy could feel the hearts of the people in the crowd going out to her.

"I'm so sorry," Kathy said suddenly. "I killed him."

What? Roxy's heart started beating too fast. It felt like everyone in the crowd took a sharp intake of breath.

"I did." She put her hands up in the air. "I thought it was the right thing to do at the time, but it wasn't. I did it because I have a huge amount of debt, and I wanted his money. I knew he had left all his money to me. I was blinded, totally blinded, by worry about my future. But now I see . . . I can't bring him back. I was crazy! I must have lost my mind! But I did it. I did. And I am so, so sorry." She broke down, sobbing hysterically.

Roxy was pushed from behind. As he passed her, she saw Detective Johnson barging his way to the front. The shove shook Roxy and propelled her into action.

"No!" she shouted. She pushed past the detective, her slight frame allowing her to weave more quickly through the crush of people in front of the stage. She rushed up the steps and onto the platform, wrenching the microphone from Kathy's hand.

Kathy launched herself at her. "Give that back!"

But Roxy wouldn't. She was standing in front of hundreds and hundreds of people, but she gripped the mic all the tighter and jerked it away from Kathy long enough to say, "She's lying! Kathy didn't kill Dash! Derek did! Dash's brother! Kathy's other son! She's only confessing to protect him!" She pointed to Detective Johnson. "Arrest him!"

Johnson had stopped amid the crowd. He didn't move. The throng fell into a silence so deep that Roxy felt she might drown in it. The heat of embarrassment rose to her cheeks.

"Detective!" Roxy hollered almost pleading now. There was a sudden movement in the crowd, and she spotted Derek. Roxy pointed, her forefinger straight and stiff. "That's him! Somebody! Anybody!"

"It's not true!" Kathy cried. "It was me! Not Derek!"

Chaos ensued. Derek, who had been watching the stage, attempted to bolt from the crowd.

"Get him!" Roxy shouted.

The crowd started roaring. Some people were stunned and let Derek through while others tried to grab him. Far from his usual lethargic self, Derek proved to be as quick as a fox and wriggled out of their grasp.

"No! No!" shouted Kathy above the crowd. "He hasn't done anything wrong!"

Derek feinted and dodged his way around the throng, but eventually, several burly men linked arms and together they acted like a trap, encircling Derek, and preventing his escape. A cop pushed his way through the crowd to place Derek in handcuffs.

Roxy turned to Kathy. "I'm so sorry," she said, "but the truth had to . . ."

Kathy had gone purple. She lunged at Roxy and grabbed her by the neck. Her warm hands closed around Roxy's airway and squeezed. Roxy felt herself begin to lose consciousness, and she stumbled. She saw Kathy's face—three versions of it—swim in front of her eyes.

Just as the world started to go black, Kathy's grip on Roxy's neck loosened. Sam had grabbed Kathy's arms, and he pinned them behind her back while she screamed. "Derek! Derek!" She kicked out at Roxy, who fell to the floor.

"Give it up, Kathy," Sam said. He was holding her tightly and, unable to even thrash against him, she slumped, defeated. Detective Johnson arrived at his shoulder and led Kathy away.

Sam bent over Roxy, who was still lying on the floor, his dark eyes clouded with concern. He put a hand to her head. "Are you all right?"

"I think so." Roxy felt her neck gingerly. "Yes, yes, I'm good. Thank you."

She braced to push herself up, and Sam helped her to her feet.

"You really didn't want to give that speech, did you?" he said.

"I did give a speech. It just wasn't the one anyone was expecting."

CHAPTER FORTY

LATER, ROXY, SAM, Nat, Elijah, Sage, Lily, Sylvia, Ada, and Michael were gathered in the lounge of the Funky Cat, nursing hot milky drinks even though it was still only afternoon. Evangeline, after hearing about the commotion on her radio, had come back to the hotel to take care of them. They were drinking sweet hot chocolate laced with brandy and topped with whipped cream and a dusting of chocolate powder. It was going down a treat.

They watched Detective Johnson on the TV. He looked very pleased with himself. "Derek Davies has admitted to the murder of his brother, Dashiell Davies. He has confessed fully. Fratricide is a heinous crime, and our thoughts are with the rest of the family."

Sage shook her head. "I accompanied Kathy to the police station. Her soul is very damaged, poor love. She was hysterical at times, and at others, her spirit left this plane to inhabit another. She told me Derek had committed the crime to help *her*, and from guilt and a misplaced sense of maternal feeling, she confessed to it falsely. Kathy has been having financial problems and Dash had helped her a lot over the years. In the past few months though, Dash had stopped giving her money because he felt she was wasting it, and that Derek was enabling her in her bad habits. Derek was furious about this, and he killed Dash so that they'd inherit all of his money. Thing was, until Michael announced it in his tribute to Dash, Derek didn't know that Dash had given all his money away.

"Kathy had no idea that Derek killed his brother, but when she looked in Derek's brown bag, she found your note, Roxy. Once she heard Derek yell out from the crowd once he learned that Dash had donated his fortune, she figured it out."

Roxy sighed. "I'd written that I would expose him unless he confessed. I had hoped the note would encourage him to be honest, that I would flush him out, but Kathy must have got his bag by mistake after they fell on the floor." Roxy pursed her lips in frustration before continuing. "So Derek killed his brother, just for money? That's terrible."

"Yes," said Sage, looking pained. "Just awful. And poor Kathy, it will take a long time for her spirit to shed such a weight. Maybe not even in this lifetime."

"What a mess," said Roxy. "But how did Derek manage to kill Dash? They live in another state. How did he make it here, carry out the murder, and get back home without Kathy noticing he was missing. And how did we not know he was in the hotel? Surely we would have heard something? I would have heard something?"

Sage shook her head. "Kathy admitted to me that they'd come to the city to see Dash when he arrived here in New Orleans. They planned to ask him for more money. When he was killed they were staying in a rundown B&B nearby and tracking his movements because they wanted to catch him when he was away from Michael. They knew Michael wouldn't approve of what they were doing and might influence Dash against them. After Dash's death, they waited a few days to show up here so it looked like they'd come from home. But Kathy genuinely didn't know what Derek had done, I'm sure of it. Who would suspect one son of killing her other son? Kathy's bewilderment was real."

Roxy sighed again. "My goodness. I suppose Derek must have sneaked into the hotel that night, perhaps during the drama over Ada's dress. He must have hidden somewhere to wait for Dash to fall asleep before going to his room to kill him."

"So," said Nat. "Are you going to tell us, Roxy? How did you know it was Derek?"

Roxy cradled her hot chocolate. "You remember the night you were attacked, Michael? The 'Evening of Love and Light'? Kathy had said Derek was going to talk to the priest. Well, when I mentioned that to Father John he looked confused and said he'd only met Derek at the memorial. I think Derek told Kathy he was going to see Father John that night, but instead, he lay in wait for Michael and attacked him on his way back to the Hilton."

"But why did he attack me?" Michael asked.

"That boy was full of jealousy. His soul is very dark," Sage said. "Extremely dark. As dark as dark gets." She looked very grave. "We may never know what was truly in his heart."

"Wow," said Sam. "It was lucky you ended up speaking to that priest, Roxy."

"Yes," she agreed. "It proved to me that Derek was a liar. I also remembered that when he and Kathy arrived here, Sage said that Derek *knew* where Dash's room was—even though he'd supposedly never been here before."

"That's right, he did," Sage said, nodding slowly. "I got chills when I met him for the very first time. I knew something wasn't right. My intuition was talking to me, but I just wasn't sure *what* it was trying to tell me."

"He must have watched the Instagram video Michael made when they first arrived. That's how he worked out how to get to Dash's room the night he killed him," Roxy said.

"But what about the poison? We never did find out exactly what killed Dash," said Ada.

"Our food was never in the frame. Detective Johnson knew Dash had been murdered from the outset, and how. But he deliberately didn't tell us, leaving us to wonder if the food he'd eaten here was involved in some way. Johnson thought that if suspicion fell on the hotel and if the killer was one of us, they would relax if they thought the investigation was headed in the wrong direction. He thought they would make a mistake and reveal themselves. I can't tell you how much I didn't appreciate that tactic when he told me this afternoon. He threw the reputation of this hotel on the fire to help his case!"

"So what did Derek kill him with?" Elijah asked.

"They couldn't work it out to start with, but when he came into the kitchen this morning, Johnson saw the model airplane Derek always carried with him. Apparently, the poison consisted of noxious fumes from some kind of glue. The police think that Derek held model airplane glue to Dash's nose while he was asleep to render him unconscious and then suffocated him with his pillow."

"Ugh," Nat said grimacing.

"What a complete ass," Michael spat.

"Goodness, you're quite the detective, though," Sylvia said to Roxy.

"Oh, it's nothing. You know, I was convinced it was you at one point. Someone put a note under my door trying to implicate you. Now I think it must have been Derek."

The color drained from Sylvia's face. She shook her head. "Oh no. Really? I'm so glad you saw through that."

Roxy considered talking to her about her ex-husband and the murder case, but she was too tired to even think. "I hope you don't mind," she said to everyone, slipping off her shoes and tucking her feet under her. "I need to relax. Let's chat about other things."

"Yes," said Nat, clearing her throat. "And I'll start. Ada, I just wanted to say that I'm really sorry for speaking to you badly at times." Nat was blushing red, but to her credit, she looked up and kept eye contact. "I was really out of order, and I'm so sorry."

Ada actually smiled at her. "That's very gracious of you, Nat. Thank you. Let's talk no more about it. It's all forgotten." Ada reached out and clasped Nat's hand. Nat responded with a squeeze and a smile.

"I will ask Archangel Michael to bring healing to us all," Sage said. "He will not let us down."

"And while Archangel Michael is doing his thing, I'll do everyone's laundry for free," Sam said, standing.

"And I'll provide the beignets!" Elijah piped up. He literally bounced out of his chair.

"Well, I'm goin' home," Evangeline said. "I've had enough excitement for one day. 'Bye, y'all."

Roxy sank back into the couch, allowing the cushions to envelop her. She beamed despite her exhaustion. Harmony, peace, and the bonds of friendship had been restored, and her world was just as she liked it. Even Nefertiti jumped into her lap and stayed for a while.

Ada, Sylvia, Lily, and Michael, despite coming to the

end of their stay at the Funky Cat Inn, seemed reluctant to leave. They continued to chat with Sage, Nat, Roxy, Sam, and Elijah all through the evening and well into the night, talking about their lives, their hopes, their dreams, their careers, their families, what they would do next, and how much they had enjoyed their stay, murder notwithstanding. It was a long, meaningful, and expansive discussion; social media wasn't mentioned once.

CHAPTER FORTY-ONE

ROXY, SAGE, AND Nat sat together in Roxy's tiny office. Sage sat on a stool beside Roxy in the office chair. They were staring intently at Sage's laptop screen. Nat lounged on the floor, sprawled out on a beanbag, which suited her just fine.

"Well, it's not *all* terrible," said Roxy, checking the hotel's Instagram page. "We've gone from 5,000 fans to 105,000!"

"That will translate into plenty more bookings," said Sage, crisply. She even *sounded* different when she was talking about business. "Visibility is key here. We need to appear *everywhere*. The more followers we have, the better."

There was a knock on the door, and Sam poked his head in. "Hello, ladies."

Sage briefly raised her eyes from the screen. Nat waved. Only Roxy looked directly at Sam. "Hi Sam."

"Roxy, can I have a word?"

"Sure." Roxy waited patiently for Sam to continue.

"Outside," he said.

"Oh, okay." Roxy pushed herself out from behind the desk and went out into the hallway where Sam stood.

"Look, I wondered, um, well, if . . ." Sam trailed off.

"Yes?" Roxy prompted. There was tension in the air, definitely tension.

"If, well, if you were alright." Sam's voice gained strength. "You know, after the other day. I mean, Kathy strangled you. That can't have been fun."

"Well, no, no, it wasn't. But you stopped her, and thank you for that. Things would have been a lot worse if not for you, but I'm fine now."

"Oh, right, well." Sam looked down at his feet before raising his head and trying again. "But you're not injured, or scared, losing sleep? I'd understand if you were. You nearly blacked out."

"No, no, I'm fine, thanks." Roxy was trembling now. Why did she do that around Sam? She remembered the vow she had made to herself. She would not get involved. Not with Sam, not with anyone. It would be unprofessional of her, and she still didn't know if she trusted him completely. And besides, she didn't have the time. "Anyhow, was there anything else?"

Sam looked directly at her. He was resolute now, having seemingly made a decision. "Just the laundry. I came for the laundry."

Roxy went back to her office where Sage and Nat were chatting about the relative merits of the different social media platforms.

"But, Sage, Instagram is where the kids go. Facebook is for old folks."

"Sylvia's followers aren't kids, and they're on Instagram, sweet petal. And look how many Facebook fans we have— 65,000!"

Roxy laughed. "I hope everyone's doing okay. Shall we check up on them?"

"Oh, yes, great idea!" said Nat. She got up off her beanbag and stood behind them.

"Let's try Lily first," Roxy said.

Sage navigated to Lily Vashchenko's Instagram page. "Aha!" Roxy said. "She *did* get the Hilton Hotel deal!" There was picture after picture of Lily posing in front of the Hilton, wearing Hilton-branded slippers, in front of the Hilton-branded pool. If it had Hilton on it, Lily was posing with it, on it, or next to it.

"Good for her," said Nat. "She really wanted that deal. It's all she could talk about when we were walking to Dash's party."

"Dash really wanted it too," Roxy said sadly.

"What about Sylvia?" said Nat.

Sage typed in *Sylvia Walters*. Nothing came up. "That's strange," said Roxy. "She's not on there."

"Do you think she deactivated?" said Nat. "She *can't* have!"

Sage closed her eyes. "Search for her *real* name," she said.

Roxy gasped. "What was it again? . . . Oh . . . erm . . . Oh, yes! Helen Matheson." Sage typed the name in. Roxy's heart was beating hard. "Oh my goodness, Sage, you're right!"

Sage clicked through to the profile. Before, Sylvia's Instagram feed had been full of well-curated pictures of lifestyle and travel. It was beautiful, for sure, but there was nothing particularly adrenaline pumping about it.

And now? Her profile picture was one of her standing alongside Oprah!

"No way!" Nat said.

"Uh-huh!" Roxy responded, finding it hard to believe herself. *"The truth will set you free!"* Roxy read from the page. *"Tell your story—the good, the bad, and the ugly. Learn from your mistakes, and speak your truth. Fight for justice!"*

Sage broke out into a beautiful smile. "This has been a learning experience for us all. Truly transformative. I vividly remember the reading I gave her. I could *feel* some inner tragedy had not been expressed. Often, I can tell exactly what a person has been through in life. I can look at them, and I *feel* their story. I see images, hear voices.

"But in her case, I didn't get anything in particular. She'd hidden her story well, somewhere no one could see or sense it; somewhere where even *she* would not see or sense it. It was buried so, so deeply. But unfortunately, when we bury our story, we bury our soul with it. She was walking around a shell of a person, always worried, always looking over her shoulder. And her throat chakra was completely blocked. It was surrounded by dark, damp energy. Having a cover story will do that to you."

Sage paused for a moment and tipped her head to one side. "You know when you try to relax, but you have a test the next day, and you haven't studied for it, and you feel disaster looming? She was living her whole *life* like that, never able to relax. Her poor soul must have been *so* tired." Sage peered at the screen and smiled. "Not anymore, though. Look at those eyes. I see joy, relief, and freedom. And a picture with Oprah? You have to be putting out some special energy into the Universe to achieve that!"

Roxy laughed. "That's fantastic. I want to find out more about what Sylvia . . . sorry, *Helen's* doing right now." Sage hit up Google and typed in "Helen Matheson." There was a Wikipedia page stating that she *had* been to jail for the death of her husband and was now using her platform to campaign for justice and help domestic violence victims.

"She has found her purpose," Sage said. She paused. "What about Ada Okafor? Let's see what she's doing." Sage searched for Ada and quickly found her profile.

"Oh, her last post is from a while ago!" Roxy pointed at the picture on her account. Ada was wearing a white coat. "Look, she's gone back to medicine!" Roxy clicked on the photo and up came the caption. *"I'm back in medical school, training to become a surgeon. Thank you, Instagram, for the fun times! See you in seven years!"*

Sage smiled at that too. "She's realized there are more important things than Versace limited editions."

"Thank goodness for that," Nat said. "I hope Michael's holding up okay," she added.

"He sure is." Sage grinned. "I don't need to check Instagram for that. He's always talking to Dr. Jack, and he's even thinking of apprenticing with him in spiritual matters. It would all be done online of course. Michael is traveling all over the world as he honors Dash's memory. Check out his pictures. You'll see!"

Roxy typed *Michael & Dash* into the bar and found their Instagram page. It was full of pictures of Michael here, there, and everywhere. In each picture, Michael held a large photograph of Dash. There were pictures of him with street children, on boats in the Caribbean, in soup kitchens, and at the top of skyscrapers.

Roxy clicked on one of the pictures. Michael was standing on a platform, an amazing view over London stretched out behind him.

Dash always said the sky was the limit. Now I'm in the

sky, in one of the tallest buildings in Europe. I'm toasting you with a glass of champagne, Dash. I'm living it up, just for you! Roxy read it out, and then they settled into a comfortable, bittersweet silence until the laptop suddenly went *ding!*

"Ooh, look! We've got a message!" Roxy said. She clicked on her inbox.

"It's from *The Magnificent Luxury Travel Show!*" said Nat peering over Roxy's shoulder.

Roxy shook her head. "It's probably just a scam."

"No, it's not!" said Nat. "It's a great TV show! It's total vacation porn."

"Nat!" Roxy said, swatting her. She opened the message and read.

Dear Roxy Reinhardt,

We have watched how you handled recent events at your hotel with grace and poise.

We love the look of the cuisine you serve, and the spiritual, historical, and cultural events you organize for your guests.

We would like to feature you in one of our shows. Please contact our scheduling producer at your earliest convenience at the email address below.

Yours sincerely,

Tiffany Schuster

Executive Producer

"Yes! I told you we would be on TV soon," said Nat, punching the air. "Oh my goodness, this is like a dream! Roxy, this is worth thousands in publicity. You've made it!"

Roxy couldn't believe her eyes. She looked out of her office door through to the lobby. In the room beyond, she could see the table that Nat had brought back from the flea market they had visited with Lily in Sam's Rolls. When Nat had got ahold of the table, it had been scratched and faded, one leg was wobbly and the side detail was caked with grime. Now, the deep mahogany finish was smooth and shiny, the fine filigree detail exposed, the wobbly leg fixed. Set on top of the table was her other flea market find—a dramatic two-foot-high gold statue of a woman. She was a dramatic figure; her hair flowed behind her, her long dress twisted around her body. In her hands were a bow and arrow, her elbow pulled back as she took aim, her intense gaze focused on her prey. Every time Roxy looked at the statue, she felt a thrill course through her body. It inspired her. The woman was powerful, determined, a servant to no one. That was just how Roxy wanted to be.

"Is this for real?" Roxy said, finally.

Sage flashed her a grin and gave her a hug. "You bet, honey."

"I can't believe it."

"Well, you better believe it, mate," Nat said. "'Cuz, it's happening. You better hold on, Rox. You're going to be famous!"

Thank you for reading *New Orleans Nightmare!* I hope you love Roxy and her gang as much as I do. The next book in the Roxy series continues her story as she finds herself in the midst of yet more mayhem.

A sinister séance. A mysterious murder. A killer with a taste for the occult....

Can Roxy narrow down the suspects, free her friend, and get back home in time to feed her cat? And more impor-

tantly, can she expose the killer before another victim joins the spirit world? Get your copy of Louisiana Lies from Amazon now! Louisiana Lies is FREE in Kindle Unlimited.

To find out about new books, sign up for my newsletter: https://www.alisongolden.com

If you love the Roxy Reinhardt mysteries, you'll also love the sweet, funny *USA Today* bestselling Reverend Annabelle Dixon series featuring a madcap, lovable lady vicar whose passion for cake is matched only by her desire for justice. The first in the series, *Death at the Cafe* is available for

purchase from Amazon. Like all my books, *Death at the Cafe* is FREE in Kindle Unlimited.

If you're looking for a detective series with twisty plots and characters that feel like friends, binge read the *USA Today* bestselling Inspector Graham series featuring a new and unusual detective with a phenomenal memory and a tragic past. The first in series, *The Case of the Screaming Beauty*, is available for purchase from Amazon and FREE in Kindle Unlimited.

If you're looking for something edgy and dangerous, root for Diana Hunter as she seeks justice after a devastating crime destroys her family. Start following her journey in this non-stop series of suspense and action. The first book in the series, Snatched is available to buy on Amazon and is FREE in Kindle Unlimited.

I hugely appreciate your help in spreading the word about *New Orleans Nightmare,* including telling a friend. Reviews help readers find books! Please leave a review on your favorite book site.

Turn the page for an excerpt from the next book in the Roxy Reinhardt series, *Louisiana Lies...*

LOUISIANA LIES

USA TODAY BESTSELLING AUTHOR

ALISON GOLDEN WITH
HONEY BROUSSARD

LOUISIANA LIES
CHAPTER ONE

ROXY SLID HER body over the smooth silky, supple leather. It responded to her like a glove, molding itself to fit her form. In front, a length of polished walnut gleamed so brightly that Roxy's face reflected back at her while under her feet was carpet so thick and soft, she felt as though her feet were suspended in midair. It was always a treat for Roxy to ride in Sam's Rolls Royce. She wasn't a very materialistic person, but even so, she couldn't help but enjoy the experience of luxury.

Sam was apologetic every time they got in it. "Just my little extravagance," he'd say, going a little red.

"Well, we certainly make a scene," said Roxy. As they cruised along, people turned to look at them as they drove by. She looked out the windows at the mash-up of sleek modern buildings created from chrome and glass, and the traditional, colorful, ornate Louisiana architecture that comprised New Orleans.

Sam grinned. "That's NOLA for you. Scenes galore."

"Yep," said Roxy. "I don't think I'll ever get used to it. And the people! I can't believe one of my best friends is an *actual* spiritualist, and we're on our way to meet one of our guests who's conducting a séance! How surreal is that?"

Sam laughed. "I wouldn't have it any other way. Makes for unpredictable, exciting times. So, tell me more about your guest. The big cheese."

"Her name is Meredith Romanoff," said Roxy. "A spiritual medium and psychic. She's very well respected and famous in her circles. At least that's what Dr. Jack said."

"So what is she doing here?"

"She's holding a series of events. Tonight's just a small one for private clients, but tomorrow she's got a huge public workshop. Over a thousand people are going. It's being held at one of the hotel conference centers, but she prefers to stay in smaller, more personable surroundings, which is why she's made a reservation with us. They booked out the *Funky Cat* even though there's only three of them. She's visiting with her husband and her assistant."

"But why are we meeting them at the botanica?"

"They were going to check in first, but traffic was bad coming into the city, and they ran out of time. So I said we'd pick up their luggage and take it back to their rooms so that it's all ready for them when they arrive."

"Always going the extra mile, hey Roxy?"

She smiled. "That's me, Nothing's-Too-Much-Trouble Roxy."

Sam smoothly pulled his maroon classic car right in front of the botanica. The magical supplies store was housed in an old, converted, shotgun-style building right in the middle of a commercial district. It wasn't grand, and it looked out of place among the sleek, modern structures that surrounded it, but it was even more eye-catching thanks to its color. The wooden boards were deep indigo, and the intricate metal fretwork that decorated the frontage was painted gold. The storefront was separated from the sidewalk by a small porch and was dominated by a huge picture window that displayed a selection of the wares stocked inside.

Crystals, oracle card sets, skulls, candles and all kinds of herbs and powders in jars filled the window to bursting. Roxy often thought that Dr. Jack could hold a scavenger hunt based on the window display alone. Roxy and Sam went inside and found a cluster of people browsing the store. A pile of bags and cases was stacked by the door.

"Hi, there!" Roxy said brightly. "We've come to . . ."

"*No,*" Dr. Jack said firmly to the woman standing in front of him, his purple face matching his velour three-piece suit. Dr. Jack loved to dress flamboyantly, and sometimes even threaded beads into his graying beard, but now he was exhibiting something much more conventional—fury. "That is absolutely unethical, and I condemn it 100%!" he cried.

"How dare you?" the woman in front of him shouted back. She pointed a thin, bony finger at Dr. Jack. It reminded Roxy of a bird's claw. She knew immediately that the woman was Meredith Romanoff.

"You presume to tell me—*ME*—that you condemn such a huge aspect of my work? Well, *that's* a fine welcome!" Meredith Romanov's soft blonde hair shook as did the ruffles that decorated the front of her blouse. The blouse stretched over her ample chest while the tassels that hung from the hem of her long skirt and which spread over her stout hips trembled. Roxy was struck by how Meredith's hands seemed at odds with her body.

In the photograph Roxy had seen, Meredith had looked as though butter wouldn't melt in her mouth, but the Meredith now in front of her offered a very different impression. Her face was red; her mouth twisted in an ugly, tortured line. She was spitting fire. Butter would be reduced to a runny puddle inside a second in the face of such an onslaught.

"Please, Meredith," a man next to her said in a placating, soothing voice. It was like he was speaking to a young child. "Now, now." The man's bald head shone under the store lights, and his cheeks were bright pink. A pair of gold spectacles hung on a slim gold chain around his neck. He dabbed his brow with a folded, pristine white handkerchief. His pressed khaki slacks were perfect. The elegantly crumpled linen shirt he wore, the sleeves rolled up neatly, indicated that sometime earlier today he had anticipated some kind of heat, but perhaps not this kind.

"Please refrain from doing this now," Roxy heard him say. "You must put yourself in the right frame of mind for your session." The man enunciated all his words with glass-cut precision. His appearance and upper-crust demeanor made him the type of person that Roxy usually felt deeply intimidated by, but he was talking to Meredith so gently that Roxy found it impossible to be scared of him.

"I can get in the right frame of mind instantly," Meredith spat. Her voice was hard. She took a deep breath, and her next words were far more measured. She delivered them with a silky veneer to her tone. "But I suppose you're right, darling. Sometimes you do talk absolute trash, but on occasion you make sense. This is one of them."

The man rolled his eyes and smiled. He chuckled. "Thank you for the high praise, darling."

Meredith caught sight of Roxy staring at her, Sam behind her. She did a double-take and immediately assumed a warm, friendly expression. "Oh, hello," she said with a smile. Roxy wasn't sure it was genuine. "You must be

. . . aren't you from the cute little hotel? Oh, I can't remember your name, I'm ever so sorry."

"It's Roxy," Roxy said brightly. "Roxy Reinhardt. This is . . ." She reached out to introduce Sam.

"I'm Sam," the tall man interjected simply, nodding at the gathered group. His shirt stretched around his broad shoulders as he folded his arms. "We know you're about to begin your meeting, so we won't disturb you. We came to pick up your bags and take them back to the hotel."

Meredith looked Sam up and down admiringly. She winked at Roxy. "What an attractive couple you make."

"Oh, we're not a couple," Roxy said quickly, feeling heat rush to her cheeks.

Meredith laughed. "Not *yet*. But I guarantee you the universe is aligning and then, well, you'll see. Now, yes, please take the bags. That would be wonderful. Thank you."

"I'll help," a young man said as he walked over to the pile of bags by the door. He had a very soft young face, red hair, and freckles. Roxy hadn't even noticed him until he spoke. He was very slight and short, and his presence was so unassuming that he was almost invisible. Roxy wondered if he was Meredith's son. He looked about the right age. "Is that okay, Meredith?" the young man asked, immediately disabusing Roxy of her theory. Her son would have called her "Mom."

"No, no, it isn't, George," Meredith snapped. "You need to be focusing on your responsibilities, getting things ready."

"Actually, I have already . . ."

"Well, then, get your mind right and meditate," said Meredith. She was terse and abrupt again. "I've told you before, you have a tendency to allow yourself to be over-whelmed by vast amounts of other people's energies, and then you don't come through as a clear channel. Anyone who needs something, you want to help. Stop being so soft and focus on what *you* have to do. You're not here to save the world or to be a 'nice guy,' you're here for a very specific purpose. And that is to help *me*." Meredith caught sight of Roxy staring at her again. "And all those lovely people we are trying to help."

Watching Meredith, Roxy felt humiliated on George's behalf, but the pleasant young man smiled. "Yes, you're right, Meredith," he said. "I'll go in the back room right away and cleanse the energies." He disappeared.

"That's more like it," Meredith said, tight-lipped. "Sorry about that, Roxy. That was George, my assistant. And this is Charles, my husband. And *this* is Terah, my old school friend." Meredith walked over to a woman browsing the racks of scented candles. She put her arm around the woman's shoulders. "We are catching up for the first time in forty years! Can you believe that?" Terah stiffened at Meredith's embrace. She wore a black eye patch over her left eye, the strap reaching over her ears and disappearing beneath her shoulder-length straight mousey hair. Terah nodded at Roxy. "We're still waiting for one more person to arrive, a private client of mine. This is Dr. Jack, of course, but I believe you are already acquainted," Meredith finished.

Jack was still hovering, his arms folded across his chest, two creases between his eyes indicating his mood. Roxy was very aware of him. He was not radiating his usual calm, accepting aura, and she felt a little anxious. Meredith's husband Charles, the man with the glasses on the gold chain, gave Roxy a friendly nod and a small smile.

"Hello, Charles, Dr. Jack, Terah. I hope you're looking forward to a good evening," said Roxy nodding at them all.

"We'll take the bags now and see you later back at the *Funky Cat Inn.*" She turned to Sam, who, his face expressionless, picked up two heavy cases and took them outside to the car.

To get your copy of *Louisiana Lies* visit the link below:
https://www.alisongolden.com/louisiana-lies

"Your emails seem to come on days when I need to read them because they are so upbeat."
- Linda W -

For a limited time, you can get the first books in each of my series - *Chaos in Cambridge, Hunted* (exclusively for subscribers - not available anywhere else), *The Case of the Screaming Beauty, and Mardi Gras Madness* - plus updates about new releases, promotions, and other Insider exclusives, by signing up for my mailing list at:

https://www.alisongolden.com/roxy

TAKE MY QUIZ

What kind of mystery reader are you? Take my thirty second quiz to find out!

https://www.alisongolden.com/quiz

BOOKS IN THE ROXY REINHARDT MYSTERIES

Mardi Gras Madness

New Orleans Nightmare

Louisiana Lies

Cajun Catastrophe

COLLECTIONS

Books 1-3

Mardi Gras Madness

New Orleans Nightmare

Louisiana Lies

FEATURING INSPECTOR DAVID GRAHAM

The Case of the Screaming Beauty

The Case of the Hidden Flame

The Case of the Fallen Hero

The Case of the Broken Doll

The Case of the Missing Letter

The Case of the Pretty Lady

The Case of the Forsaken Child

The Case of Sampson's Leap

The Case of the Uncommon Witness

FEATURING REVEREND ANNABELLE DIXON

Chaos in Cambridge (Prequel)

Death at the Café

Murder at the Mansion

Body in the Woods

Grave in the Garage

Horror in the Highlands

Killer at the Cult

Fireworks in France

Witches at the Wedding

ABOUT THE AUTHOR

Alison Golden is the *USA Today* bestselling author of the Inspector David Graham mysteries, a traditional British detective series, and two cozy mystery series featuring main characters Reverend Annabelle Dixon and Roxy Reinhardt. As A. J. Golden, she writes the Diana Hunter thriller series.

Alison was raised in Bedfordshire, England. Her aim is to write stories that are designed to entertain, amuse, and calm. Her approach is to combine creative ideas with excellent writing and edit, edit, edit. Alison's mission is simple: To write excellent books that have readers clamouring for more.

Alison is based in the San Francisco Bay Area with her husband and twin sons. She splits her time between London and San Francisco.

For up-to-date promotions and release dates of upcoming books, sign up for the latest news here: https://www.alisongolden.com/roxy.

For more information:
www.alisongolden.com
alison@alisongolden.com

facebook.com/alisongolden.books

x.com/alisonjgolden

instagram.com/alisonjgolden

THANK YOU

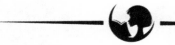

Thank you for taking the time to read *New Orleans Nightmare*. If you enjoyed it, please consider telling your friends or posting a short review. Word of mouth is an author's best friend and very much appreciated.
Thank you,

Printed in the USA
CPSIA information can be obtained
at www.ICGtesting.com
LVHW040114290524
781666LV00030B/579